The Squaring of a Heart

*A Novel of Love, Second Chances, and the
Small Town That Refused to Give Up*

Cameron Lane

Stone House Editions

2025

The Squaring of a Heart

A Novel of Love, Second Chances, and the Small Town That Refused to Give Up

© 2025 **Cameron Lane**

Published by **Stone House Editions**
Stories of the Heart, the Spirit, and the Unknown

eBook ISBN: 979-8-9992336-2-2
Paperback ISBN: 979-8-9992336-9-1

For inquiries or permissions, visit:
CameronLaneBooks.com

Printed in the United States of America and other locations worldwide.

Table of Contents

For the towns that time almost forgot —
and the people who wouldn't let it.
This is for your storefronts, your festivals, your second chances.

Chapter 1

The Return

The train slowed as it pulled into Marigold Station, its whistle slicing through the heavy late-summer air. Sophie Caldwell tightened her grip on the worn leather strap of her laptop bag, heart pounding as the familiar shape of the station emerged: cracked pavement, a rusting "Welcome to Marigold" sign hanging at a crooked angle, its paint bleached and peeling from years of sun.

Fifteen years, and nothing had changed.

The doors hissed open. Sophie stepped down onto the platform, her heels clicking against warped wood slats, and inhaled deeply. The scent hit her first — fresh-cut grass mingling with faint barbecue smoke from somewhere downtown. The smell of home. And yet it didn't feel like home at all.

Her chest tightened, sharp and sudden, as memories crashed over her: her mother's laugh on a summer afternoon, the sting of gossip that followed them out of town, the hollow stillness of the house they left behind. The way neighbors had turned away at the grocery store, whispers trailing them like shadows. This place hadn't just shaped her — it had left its mark in wounds that never fully healed.

Marigold. The town that had broken her family. The town that had broken her heart.

A train horn in the distance, fading into silence. Sophie squared her shoulders. This wasn't about nostalgia. This was about keeping a promise. One she'd made at her mother's bedside, in those final, fragile moments.

"I'll bring it back to life, Mom," she'd whispered, voice cracking. "I'll fix what they broke."

The square had been the heart of Marigold once. But as Sophie walked down Main Street, suitcase wheels bumping over cracked sidewalks, the decay was impossible to miss. Empty storefronts with dusty "For Lease" signs. The old movie theater's marquee missing letters so it read "The G eat Escape." A place clinging to its bones.

She passed Lenny's Diner — boarded up. The ice cream parlor where she'd shared sundaes with her dad — gone, windows papered over. Even the bookstore where she'd hidden from the world had given up the ghost.

A few townspeople watched her pass, eyes filled with that small-town blend of curiosity and caution. Mrs. Holcomb, who'd once taught her piano, stared from the pharmacy window, lips pursed. A pair of teenagers slouched against the post office wall, eyeing her with suspicion and something like hope.

She kept her gaze ahead, though the weight of their stares pressed on her.

Sophie stopped at the edge of the square. The once-proud fountain in the center stood dry and crumbling, its basin littered weeds. Overgrown planters framed broken brick walkways. A beer bottle glinted beneath a bench; a frayed sneaker dangled from a lamppost, swinging like a forgotten flag.

"This is it," she murmured, her voice swallowed by the humid air. "Ground zero."

The Fort and the Storm

Sophie's gaze drifted toward the ancient oak at the corner of Main and Willow. And in that moment, memory took her.

She was nine, knees scraped raw, tears hot on her cheeks after the Lawson twins had cornered her by the swing set. Cal had found her crouched beneath that very tree, a defiant little protector in hand-me-down sneakers and a too-big flannel shirt.

"Don't let 'em see you cry," he'd whispered, glancing over his shoulder like he could hold the world at bay. "They don't deserve it."

He'd offered her his peanut butter sandwich — half-mashed but shared without hesitation — and as the summer storm rolled over the fields, they'd watched the sky darken together.

"Someday I'll build you a fort here," Cal had promised, his voice low with certainty. "Big enough no one can bother you."

Sophie had believed him. Back then, she'd believed in forts and treehouses, in promises made under storm clouds.

But the fort never came. The storms did.

Sophie blinked, the present rushing back. The oak's branches reached like weary arms toward the sky. The empty square spread before her like a battlefield, waiting for its fight.

Her pulse quickened — part dread, part determination. The square wasn't just neglected — it felt abandoned by hope itself.

A voice behind her broke the stillness.

"You're Sophie Caldwell, aren't you?"

She turned. A man stood there — tall, broad-shouldered, sun-browned arms crossed over a chest that had filled out with years of real work. His eyes, the color of storm clouds, met hers without flinching.

Cal Bennett.

The name hit her before the recognition did. He was taller now, broader, his stance more grounded — like the very square he fought to protect. Local business owner. Single father. The man who'd kept Marigold's last flicker of pride alive when others gave up. Once, he'd been the quiet boy sketching bikes and treehouses in his notebook's margins, the boy who'd helped her up when she fell off the monkey bars. Now, that boy was gone — replaced by a man who looked like he could hold up the whole town with his bare hands.

"Well, look who the train dragged back in," Cal said, his arms crossing like a gate slammed shut.

Sophie managed a half-smile. "And you must be the welcoming committee."

He didn't smile back. "If you're here to tear down what's left of this town, you'll have a fight on your hands."

Her pulse quickened — not with fear, but with the familiar rush of a challenge. She'd stared down CEOs and city officials in glass towers without flinching. But there was something about Cal's quiet certainty, the way he rooted himself like he belonged to this place, that rattled her more than any power broker ever had.

"I'm not here to destroy anything," she said evenly. "I'm here to help."

"Big city help? We've seen what that gets us."

The words stung more than she expected.

Cal turned, striding across the square like he owned every inch of it. His battered work truck groaned as he climbed in, tools clanging a final warning. The engine's growl lingered long after the dust settled.

Sophie exhaled slowly, the weight of memory, expectation — and something else she couldn't name — settling on her shoulders.

The Ghosts of Marigold

She checked into the only inn still open — the Marigold House, its porch sagging slightly, its paint in need of rescue. The innkeeper, Mrs. Clemens, had seemed more surprised than pleased to see her, but offered a key and a room that smelled faintly of lavender and mothballs.

That night, Sophie couldn't sleep. The town's silence pressed against the window glass, thick and oppressive. She sat at the little desk in her room, laptop open, sketches and figures illuminated by the soft glow of the screen. Plans. Designs. Financial models. She'd come prepared.

But plans couldn't account for the weight of memory.

Her mother's voice echoed in her mind. Her father's laughter, before everything fell apart. The funeral. The whispered judgments. The day she left, vowing never to return.

Once, this town had felt like a promise. Now, it felt like unfinished business.

A dog barked somewhere in the night. Sophie shut the laptop and went to the window, looking down on Main Street. The square lay in shadow, the fountain a ghost of its former self.

And then she saw him.

Cal.

Standing by the fountain, hands in his pockets, head bowed. A solitary figure in the dark, as if keeping vigil over what remained.

Something in Sophie's chest ached. She closed the curtain and went to bed, though sleep wouldn't come until just before dawn.

Morning in Marigold

The sun rose hot and unrelenting. Sophie dressed in jeans and boots, hair pulled back, ready to face the day.

She walked the square, taking notes, snapping photos. Her plans were ambitious — too ambitious, maybe. But the town deserved more than half-measures.

At the café, she ordered coffee and endured the cautious stares of townspeople. The barista, a young woman with a warm smile, handed over the cup.

"Welcome to Marigold," she said softly.

Sophie blinked, then nodded. "Thanks."

Collision Course

By mid-morning, Sophie found herself back at the fountain, measuring distances, imagining what could be.

"I thought you were here to help," Cal's voice drawled from behind her.

She turned. He stood there, posture rigid, one hand hooked loosely on his belt — like he was bracing for a blow, but his gaze held more curiosity than challenge this time.

"I am," she said.

"Most people who want to help start by listening."

Sophie hesitated, then lowered her tape measure. "Okay. I'm listening."

Cal looked surprised — but only for a moment.

"Come on," he said. "I'll show you what you're up against."

Together, they walked the square, Cal pointing out hidden faults, stories behind empty buildings, people who'd left or given up. He spoke of his family's hardware store — opened by his grandfather, passed down to his father, now boarded up and gathering dust; of the bakery that closed after its owner's heart attack; of the library where his mother once worked, its windows cracked and dark.

By the time they finished, the sun was high and Sophie's notebook was filled with more than numbers and sketches. It held names, histories, wounds she hadn't seen before.

She looked at Cal. "You really care about this place."

"I was born here. I've got skin in the game."

"So do I."

Their eyes met — and for the first time, the tension between them softened.

"This isn't just a project for me," Sophie said quietly. "It's personal."

Cal nodded slowly. "Then maybe we're on the same side after all."

Maybe.

The Meeting That Divided the Room

Two nights after her arrival, Sophie stood at the front of the community center — the former Grange Hall where generations had gathered for pancake breakfasts, talent shows, and wedding dances. Now the air was thick with dust and distrust.

Folding chairs scraped harshly against scuffed floors as people settled in — farmers in work-stained jeans, retirees in ball caps, young families clutching hope and doubt in equal measure. Sophie's heart pounded, but her voice was steady.

"I know what this town meant. What it can mean again. I'm not here to erase Marigold's past — I'm here to honor it while we build a future."

A murmur rippled through the room. Sheriff Tolliver — retired, but still a force — shifted forward. "And what's it gonna cost us? More outsiders coming in? Folks who don't care, just want a quick buck?"

"We've seen plans before, Miss Caldwell," added Marla Jensen, arms folded tight. "Fancy diagrams, big promises. Then nothing but boarded-up shops and more For Lease signs."

Sophie's throat tightened. Before she could reply, Cal's voice cut through the rising tension — quiet but firm.

"She's not wrong to want more for this place. We all should."

Heads turned. Cal stepped into the light, his presence grounding the room.

"But wanting's not enough," he added, gaze flicking to Sophie. "Marigold's been burned before. We've earned our right to ask hard questions."

Sophie nodded, meeting him halfway. "Then ask them. I'm not afraid of answers."

The silence that followed felt like a truce — fragile, but real.

Cal's Night at the Workbench

That night, long after the town hall, Cal sat alone in his workshop. The air smelled of sawdust, motor oil, and the faint trace of coffee gone cold. His hands — cracked, calloused, raw from work — rested on the scarred wood of the bench.

In front of him lay a photo: Cal at twenty-two, grinning awkwardly, cradling baby Emma like she was made of glass. The girl was 10 now, taller by the day, and the reason Cal hauled himself out of bed every morning.

He exhaled, shoulders heavy. He thought of the promises he'd made — to his girl, to this town. The porch he'd patched for old Mrs. Dorsey. The roof he'd fixed for the church. The hours spent trying to hold Marigold together one nail, one board at a time.

And still, it slipped through his fingers.

Cal picked up a block of cedar and his carving knife. Slowly, methodically, he began to shape it, shaving away curls of wood. A small thing, but solid. Tangible. Something he could finish, at least.

The knife whispered against the grain as the night deepened around him, and somewhere in the quiet,

Cal allowed himself the smallest measure of hope.

Before the Council

The air inside Marigold's town hall smelled of furniture polish, old paper, and barely concealed frustration. Sophie sat at the long oak table, her laptop open in front of her, a sleek machine out of place among the scuffed wood and yellowed maps on the walls. Sunlight filtered through tall, arched windows, pooling on the dusty floorboards like liquid gold. Ceiling fans stirred the thick air but did little to ease it. Around her, the council members fidgeted, cleared throats, adjusted reading glasses. The room felt like it hadn't changed in decades — the same framed portraits of former mayors, the same chipped mug on the clerk's desk, the same weight of decisions that had stalled more than they had saved.

"I appreciate your time," Sophie began, projecting calm she didn't entirely feel. "What I'm proposing isn't just renovation. It's renewal. The square can be the beating heart of Marigold again — a destination, not a detour."

She clicked the remote in her hand. The screen at the end of the room flickered to life, displaying a sleek rendering of the town square: clean lines, restored storefronts, flower beds bursting with color, the fountain once again flowing. The image was bright, hopeful — maybe too hopeful.

Murmurs rippled through the room. Some leaned in. Others leaned back, arms crossed.

Councilwoman Hester Boyd leaned forward, her gray braid swinging over one shoulder, the click of her pen loud in the quiet. "Ms. Caldwell, it's an attractive vision. But how, exactly, do you propose to fund this fantasy?"

Sophie smiled, practiced and precise. "A combination of grants, private investment, and phased development. I've already begun conversations with heritage foundations. The key is demonstrating community buy-in, which is why I'm here today. I want to partner with Marigold, not bulldoze it."

From the back of the room, Cal's voice cut through the polite chatter. "Funny. That's exactly what bulldozers say before they start digging."

Heads turned. Cal leaned against the doorway, arms crossed, his stance as stubborn as the scowl on his face. Sophie hadn't seen him enter. Typical.

"Mr. Bennett," she said, keeping her tone neutral. "Good of you to join us."

"I live here," he shot back. "Figured I should see who's planning to pave paradise."

A ripple of nervous laughter. Sophie drew a slow breath, steadying herself against the knot forming at the base of her neck.

"I'm not paving anything," she said. "I'm proposing to restore what's crumbling. You said yourself just yesterday — the square's in trouble."

Cal's gaze didn't waver. "I said it needs care, not a corporate makeover."

Sophie clicked to the next slide — a budget outline, clean and detailed. "No one's proposing chains or parking garages. The businesses would be locally owned. The contractors would be from here. Every decision, from materials to signage, would reflect Marigold's character."

Hester cleared her throat, pen tapping a restless rhythm. "What about that big developer? The one from Atlanta? They've been sniffing around for months. What makes you different?"

"I'm not them," Sophie said simply. "I'm not looking to flip this town for profit. My mother was born here. My family's roots are in that square. I want to help Marigold thrive — not turn it into a strip mall with better branding."

That got a few nods. Even Cal seemed, for a heartbeat, to soften. Then his jaw set again.

"And you're funding this out of the goodness of your heart?" he asked. "Or is there a catch we haven't heard yet?"

Sophie met his gaze head-on. "The only catch is that this doesn't work without you. Without all of you. I can bring resources, plans, connections — but Marigold has to bring its will. I'm offering a partnership, not a takeover."

Silence stretched. Sophie let it. She'd learned in boardrooms and negotiations that silence often said more than speeches.

Finally, Hester tapped her pen one last time and set it down. "We'll consider your proposal. But this council moves cautiously. You should know that."

"I respect that," Sophie said. "And I'm happy to provide more details, answer questions, whatever you need."

The Aftermath

The meeting broke up in polite murmurs. People filed out, some glancing at Sophie with curiosity, others with skepticism. Cal lingered at the doorway, watching, his expression unreadable.

When the room had emptied, he spoke. "You're good. I'll give you that. Slick slides, pretty words."

Sophie gathered her laptop, slipping it into her bag. "You think I'm lying?"

"I think you're selling something. Maybe you believe in it. Maybe you don't. But either way, it's a sale."

She moved closer, until only the width of the table separated them. "You don't know me, Cal. You think you do because of some files or because I left. But you don't. And if you're so sure I'm here to ruin Marigold, maybe stop throwing stones from the sidelines and help."

For a moment, she thought he might. His eyes softened, just enough. Then he shook his head. "Don't expect me to cheerlead a plan that could gut this town."

"I'm offering to stitch it back together."

"Some stitches leave scars," he said quietly. And then he was gone.

On the Steps

Outside, Sophie paused on the steps of town hall, letting the humid air fill her lungs. The meeting had drained her, left her throat dry from polite sparring and her heart heavier than she cared to admit. Across the square, the fountain stood as dry and cracked as ever, pigeons perched on its rim like sentries keeping watch over a kingdom long forgotten. The breeze carried a mix of scents — mown grass, fried food from somewhere down the block, and the faint sweetness of crepe myrtle blossoms.

A kid on a bike wove between the planters, tires kicking up dust, the clatter of his playing cards hitting the spokes breaking the stillness. Sophie watched him disappear down an alley, his laughter echoing briefly before being swallowed by silence again.

The Historian

A voice behind her made her start. "He's not wrong, you know."

Sophie turned, heart still racing from the surprise. A woman in her sixties stood at the bottom of the steps, silver hair cropped short, eyes sharp behind wire-rimmed glasses. She wore a faded denim shirt over a floral dress, and carried a canvas tote that sagged with the weight of books.

"Excuse me?" Sophie asked, schooling her expression into polite curiosity.

"About scars," the woman said, climbing the steps slowly but steadily. "This town's been burned before. Developers with big ideas, promises of jobs, tourists, prosperity. Never ends well. Folks here are wary. They've learned to look for the catch."

Sophie nodded, her throat tight. "I expected skepticism. I didn't expect... open hostility."

The woman huffed a soft laugh. "Marigold's like a stray dog, Ms. Caldwell. Looks rough, maybe growls when you reach out, but it's not mean. It's just been kicked too many times."

Sophie extended her hand. "Sophie Caldwell."

The woman set down her bag and shook it. Her grip was firm, her palm calloused. "Jeanine Marks. I run the historical society. And the bookstore. And I'm the secretary for the garden club. Small towns — you collect hats."

There was a twinkle in her eye despite the frank tone.

Sophie allowed herself a small smile. "Then maybe you can help me figure out how to wear mine without getting run out of town."

Jeanine's smile deepened, lines creasing the corners of her mouth. "Maybe. But don't expect a map. People here will test you. They'll see if you stick around when it's hard. That's how they decide if you're worth the trust."

Sophie crossed her arms, gazing out at the square. "I want to be worth it. I'm not here for a quick win. My mother—" Her voice caught. She cleared her throat. "My mother loved this place. I promised I'd try to save it."

Jeanine studied her for a long beat, as if weighing those words against some private scale. "You know where saving starts?"

"Where?"

"With memory." She glanced toward the square, then back. "I knew your mother, you know. Quiet fire, that woman. Shelved half the town's childhoods at that library, and probably remembered every overdue name. She'd be glad you're back."

She nodded toward the square. "Listening. That's the next step. Every building has a story. Every person does too. Before you can rebuild anything, you'd better learn what's already standing — under the paint and the rot."

Sophie sighed, the weight of the day pressing harder. "That's what Cal said. Different words, same message."

Jeanine chuckled. "He's blunt, but he's not wrong. He's the closest thing this town has to a conscience, whether he likes it or not."

A gust of wind lifted a loose strand of Sophie's hair, and she tucked it behind her ear. "I don't want to fight him."

"You don't have to," Jeanine said gently. "Just show up. Show you care for more than profit or pride. Marigold notices those things. We may be small, but we see sharp."

Sophie hesitated. "Would you — would you talk to the council? Help them see I mean well?"

Jeanine bent to pick up her tote. "I don't vouch for folks I've just met. But I'll talk. I'll listen. And if you prove yourself, I'll speak up when it matters."

There was no malice in her voice — just honesty, clear as a church bell on a cold morning.

Sophie nodded, oddly grateful for the lack of easy comfort. "Thank you. That's fair."

Jeanine adjusted the tote on her shoulder. "Come by the bookstore tomorrow. Morning's best — I get cranky after lunch."

"I'll be there."

Later That Evening

That night, Sophie walked the square alone. The day's heat had finally broken, the air cooler now, scented faintly with honeysuckle and woodsmoke from some distant porch. A breeze stirred the flags that hung limp from the lampposts, rustling the leaves in the planters and carrying the low hum of cicadas.

She moved slowly, taking it all in — the empty benches where neighbors once lingered over ice cream and gossip, the darkened storefronts whose windows reflected her shadowed face, the ghost of a town that still clung to its shape but not its spirit.

At the fountain, she stopped. The cracked stone felt cool beneath her fingertips, rough and pitted as an old scar. The night air's honeysuckle and woodsmoke scent mixed with the faint tang of rust from the fountain's dry pipes. Sophie closed her eyes and tried to summon the square's forgotten heartbeat: water catching sunlight like liquid glass, children's laughter skipping across the surface, teenagers balancing on the rim in dares of courage, lovers tossing coins and whispering promises they might have believed in. But the vision fractured, overtaken by the sharp smell of mildew, the sight of weeds clawing through the cracks, and graffiti carved deep like old wounds. The silence was no longer peaceful — it felt like absence made visible.

A sound broke the stillness — the steady rhythm of boots on brick. Sophie turned, heart quickening. From the shadows near the old theater, Cal emerged, his figure outlined by the pale glow of the streetlamp.

"I didn't expect an audience," she said, her voice soft, the night inviting honesty.

"Didn't expect to be one," he replied. His tone was quieter now, the sharp edge dulled, replaced by something more thoughtful. "Couldn't sleep. Thought I'd walk. Saw you out here, figured I'd say my piece."

Sophie folded her arms, more to steady herself than out of defense. "And what piece is that?"

He came a few steps closer, hands shoved in his pockets, gaze steady but not unkind. "You really believe you can fix this?" He swept his hand toward the square — the boarded-up shops, the empty sidewalks, the fountain that hadn't held water in years.

"I have to believe it," Sophie said after a moment. "It's the only reason I came back. If I didn't believe, I wouldn't have a reason to stay."

Cal studied her face as if trying to decide whether he could trust what he saw. "You could've stayed gone. Nobody would've blamed you for that. Least of all me."

"I tried," she admitted, the words tasting of truth. "I tried for a long time. But I couldn't shake it. This place… it's in me, whether I like it or not."

A breeze lifted her hair, and she brushed it back, suddenly self-conscious under his steady gaze.

Cal exhaled slowly. "You don't have to convince me tonight. I'm not the one you need to win over. But just… be careful. People here — they don't forget promises. And they sure as hell don't forget when promises get broken. They've been let down too many times to fall for pretty plans."

Sophie nodded, feeling the weight of his words settle over her like the night air. "I'm not here to let them down. I'm not here to let myself down, either."

For the first time, Cal smiled — a small, fleeting thing, but real. "We'll see," he said, his voice almost gentle.

And with that, he turned, the sound of his boots receding as he made his way toward his truck parked at the edge of the square. The engine rumbled to life, headlights washing the cracked square in pale gold. But Cal didn't drive off — he lingered, as if weighing some silent decision, his silhouette framed in the cab's glow. Then, slowly, the truck eased away, its taillights disappearing down Main Street, leaving only the hush of the night behind.

Sophie stood at the fountain, the square spread before her like a fractured map of old hopes and new burdens. The darkness pressed close, but so did determination. Tomorrow, she would listen harder. Work smarter. Not just speak, but act. The square didn't need another plan. It needed hands, heart — and time. And piece by piece, she would start stitching it back together.

Chapter 2

The City's Goodbye

The city hummed beneath Sophie's apartment window — sirens weaving through late-night traffic, voices rising from the sidewalk below, the sharp bark of a dog chasing shadows. The glow of neon signs painted the cracked plaster walls in streaks of pink and blue, flickering like a heartbeat out of rhythm.

Sophie stood barefoot at the window, one hand resting on the sill, watching as the night swallowed the last of the day's light. Her suitcase lay open on the bed behind her, half-filled: clothes she didn't care about anymore, faded plans that felt like relics, and a photo of her mother tucked inside an old architectural journal.

She'd told herself this was a fresh start. A chance to build something new. But standing here, looking out at the city she'd tried so hard to love, all she felt was tired.

The apartment door clicked open. Nathan stepped inside, keys jangling, the scent of cologne and city air clinging to him. He paused when he saw her, his shoulders tense beneath his tailored coat.

"You're really leaving," he said, voice too smooth, too late.

Sophie didn't turn. "I have to."

Nathan crossed the room, stopping a few feet behind her. "You could stay. We could make this work. You don't have to run back to—"

"Don't," she said quietly. "Don't make this about us. You know as well as I do, there hasn't been an 'us' for a long time."

Silence stretched, thick with everything they weren't saying.

Nathan exhaled, rubbing the back of his neck. "I guess I thought you'd change your mind."

Sophie closed her eyes for a moment, letting the sounds of the city fill the space between them. "I promised her. And I promised myself. I can't stay here, trying to fix something that's already gone. Not us. Not this place."

He hesitated, then nodded. "Then I hope you find what you're looking for."

Sophie turned at last, offering a small, sad smile. "Me too."

Nathan left without another word, the soft click of the door sounding final in the quiet.

The Last Walk

Sleep wouldn't come. The apartment felt too still, too heavy with memories of late nights and early mornings spent chasing deadlines, of laughter that had faded long before Nathan had.

So Sophie left the apartment.

The city was a patchwork of light and shadow, steam rising from manhole covers, neon bleeding into puddles that mirrored the world upside down. She passed the coffee shop that once felt like home, where baristas knew her order but not her heart. The bookstore with creaking floors where she'd lost herself in other people's stories. The little park where she'd sketched towers and plazas she thought would change the world.

All of it familiar. None of it hers anymore.

At the river, she leaned on the railing, watching dark water rush past, carrying secrets toward the sea. The skyline glowed behind her — a city she'd shaped her life around, and one that had slowly hollowed her out.

"I gave you everything I had," she whispered, as if the city might listen. And maybe it did. Maybe that was why it stayed silent.

The Final Morning

Dawn came pale and uncertain, streaking the sky with soft gold. Sophie stood at the window one last time, her suitcase packed now, the apartment stripped bare of everything that made it hers.

She watched the city wake: delivery trucks rumbling down side streets, joggers splashing through the last of the night's rain, the first scent of coffee drifting up from the café on the corner.

Her phone buzzed on the counter. Another offer — a project in a city that wasn't home, for a client who wouldn't remember her name in a year. She let it ring.

Her cab pulled up. The driver leaned on the horn, impatient. Sophie took one last look around the apartment, then stepped out, pulling the door shut behind her. The click of the latch felt like closing a chapter.

A New Promise

In the cab, as the city slid past in flashes of steel and glass, Sophie touched the photo in her bag — her mother's smile, the fountain behind them, Marigold in its best light.

Nathan's voice echoed in her mind: *You'll hate it there.*

But Sophie knew he was wrong.

She wasn't running *to* Marigold. She was running *toward* herself.

And this time, she wasn't coming back.

As the cab turned toward the train station, Sophie didn't look back. The city had given her all it could. Now Marigold — broken, waiting — would give her something harder: the chance to keep a promise.

Chapter 3

First Steps and Fault Lines

Dawn broke slowly and heavy, draping Marigold in pink and gold. From the second-story window of the Marigold House, Sophie watched the town stir to life — if it could be called that. The square looked softened in the early light, like an old photograph left too long in the sun. Less like a battlefield, more like a forgotten garden waiting for hands to tend it.

She traced the cracked sidewalks with her gaze, imagined the fountain flowing again — water sparkling in the morning sun, its soft splash filling the square the way music once had. She pictured shop windows glowing, cafés spilling laughter and jazz into the street, flower boxes bursting with color. Then the images faded, overtaken by what was: boarded doors, sagging awnings, the bitter tang of neglect that even the sweet morning air couldn't cover.

A pair of pigeons flapped down to the fountain's rim, pecking at nothing, wings stirring dust. Across the square, a boy on a rusted bike coasted through a puddle, sending up a spray that glinted like silver. Sophie watched until he vanished down an alley, leaving the square empty again, silent but for the soft creak of a shop sign in the breeze.

Beneath the quiet, tension hummed. Sophie felt it in her chest, in the weight of unfinished promises that had brought her here, in the knowledge that today wasn't just another day of plans and meetings. Today she had to begin building trust — real trust, not the polite nods of a council chamber. Without it, the square would be lost to someone else's vision. And she would have failed, not just herself, but her mother's memory.

A knock interrupted her thoughts.

Mrs. Clemens entered with a tray: coffee dark as molasses, two slices of toast browned unevenly at the edges, and a small jar of peach preserves with a torn label and sticky fingerprints along the rim.

"Thank you," Sophie said, meaning it. The small kindness felt like a bridge across the distance that had settled between her and this town.

Mrs. Clemens lingered at the window, wiping her hands on her apron, eyes following the same cracks Sophie had been studying.

"You'll forgive us if we don't roll out the welcome mat," she said finally, voice quiet but firm. "We've seen plans before. They always start the same — pretty drawings, fancy talk, big promises. But they end with empty stores, strangers owning what we built, and more out-of-towners telling us what we should be."

Sophie swallowed hard, fingers tightening around the warm mug. "I'm not here to tell Marigold what it should be. I'm here to help it become what it wants — what it *deserves* to be."

Mrs. Clemens's eyes softened, just barely. The lines at the corners of her mouth deepened, as if she wanted to believe.

"We'll see, dear," she said at last. She turned, sensible shoes clicking softly against the worn floorboards as she walked away, leaving behind the scent of coffee, the faint sweetness of peach, and the invisible weight of history that clung to the air like humidity.

Alone again, Sophie sipped her coffee and let the bitterness ground her. Below, the square waited — patient, but wary. And she knew this was no longer about designs or budgets. This was about earning back the town's heartbeat, one careful step at a time.

Marigold Books & History sat like a stubborn relic between two hollowed-out storefronts, its faded red door flanked by dusty windows crammed with old maps, yellowing flyers, and hand-lettered signs that had long lost their ink's fight against the sun. Above the door, the painted sign had weathered into ghostly outlines, but History still stood out bold, as if defying time itself.

Sophie hesitated before pushing the door open. The bell overhead let out a tired jingle — the kind that carried memories of livelier days.

Inside, the shop smelled of lemon oil, old paper, and the faint trace of pipe smoke, as if some long-gone regular still haunted the corners. Books filled every inch: shelves bowed beneath their weight, stacks rose like miniature cityscapes, paperbacks overflowed from baskets, their spines cracked and titles faded. A cat — or maybe just the idea of one — seemed to linger, though Sophie saw no sign of life beyond the books.

Jeanine Marks stood behind a scarred counter, hands busy with a pen and battered ledger. She didn't look up as Sophie entered.

"You're on time," Jeanine said, voice dry but not unkind. She wiped her hands on her apron, leaving dark smudges of ink to join a constellation of stains.

Sophie stepped closer, taking in the woman's sharp eyes behind wire-rimmed glasses, her silver hair cropped short, the way she carried herself like someone who'd outlasted more storms than she cared to count.

"I'm trying to start on the right foot," Sophie said.

Jeanine snorted, though there was a hint of a smile. "Smart. Marigold has a long memory for missteps."

She gestured to a round table near the front window, crowded with papers: faded photographs, brittle maps, notes scrawled in looping cursive. Jeanine slid a battered manila folder toward Sophie.

"Old photos. Maps. A few minutes of history, if you're willing."

Sophie opened the folder carefully, as if the contents might fall apart in her hands. The black-and-white snapshots inside were windows into another Marigold: flower baskets bursting with color along the square, townsfolk lined up for parades in their Sunday best, children laughing as they dangled their feet in the fountain's clear water, shopkeepers beaming in front of polished windows.

She ran a thumb along the edge of one photo: the fountain in full spray, a pair of kids — maybe her mother among them — balancing on the rim, daring each other not to fall in.

Jeanine busied herself at a small sideboard, pouring tea into two mismatched mugs. The kettle hissed quietly, filling the shop with steam and warmth.

"You want to build trust?" Jeanine said, setting a mug in front of Sophie. "You talk to Reed at the barbershop. He's gruff as they come, but he remembers everything — and he'll remind you of it, too. Naomi Tolliver runs the food pantry — sees where the cracks are, in the buildings and the people. And Cal."

She paused, sitting across from Sophie, her hands wrapped around her mug.

"You need Cal, whether you like it or not. His voice carries farther than he knows. Folks watch him. When he speaks, even if they grumble about it later, they listen."

Sophie looked up from the photos. "Does Cal speak for the town?"

Jeanine's laugh was soft, wry. "No one speaks for Marigold. But Cal? People know he's paid in sweat and sacrifice. They trust what he builds with his hands more than what anyone puts on paper."

She fixed Sophie with a long, assessing look.

"I don't vouch for outsiders. Never have. But I'll listen. And if you show up when it counts, if you keep showing up — maybe I'll speak up when it matters."

Outside, the square lay quiet under the morning sun, but inside the shop, something had shifted — the first crack in the wall between newcomer and native, between plan and possibility

The morning sun climbed higher, casting long shadows that stretched across the square like fingers trying to hold the place together. Sophie moved slowly, Jeanine's folder tucked under one arm, her other hand brushing lightly along chipped paint, cracked brick, rusted metal — as if touch might tell her the square's secrets better than sight.

A soft breeze stirred faded flags on the lampposts. The air smelled of warm dust, old brick, and the faint sweetness of crepe myrtle blossoms clinging to life along the park fence.

At the barbershop, Mr. Reed sat in a patch of shade beneath the overhang, polishing the glass of the old display case with slow, circular strokes. His hands, mottled with age, moved with care.

Sophie hesitated, then stepped closer.

"You're Caldwell's girl," he said, eyeing her over the rim of his glasses. His voice was rough as gravel, but not unkind — just worn by years.

"Yes, sir. Sophie."

He nodded once, setting down his rag and straightening with effort. His gaze drifted to the fountain, where pigeons pecked at weeds pushing through the cracked basin.

"That ran clean once," he said, the words heavy with memory. "Before promises dried up. Before folks stopped seeing this place as theirs."

There was no accusation in his tone, just sadness. Sophie followed his gaze, swallowing the knot rising in her throat.

"Maybe it can again," she said quietly.

Mr. Reed snorted, but there was no real bite in it. "Hope's a stubborn thing. You'll need plenty."

She left him to his polishing, his reflection blurred in the dusty glass.

In the park, a teenager in a faded ball cap worked methodically, stuffing candy wrappers and crumpled flyers into a plastic bag. Sophie approached, offering a tentative smile.

"Need a hand?"

The boy shook his head, not unkindly, just resigned.

"Nah. I got it." He jammed another handful of litter into the bag.

"Be nice if we had something to do here," he muttered, almost to himself. His voice carried the weight of too many empty summers, too many promises of improvement that had turned to dust.

Sophie watched him for a moment, heart aching. "I'm hoping to change that," she said, but he didn't look up, and she didn't press.

Near the abandoned café, the sun caught on broken glass glinting like false stars in the dirt. And in the shade of the awning, Cal's daughter, Emma, crouched low, sketchbook balanced on her knees. Her pencil flew across the page, capturing the square's worn edges — the sag of the shop rooflines, the lean of the old lamppost, the stubborn dignity in the cracked fountain.

Sophie didn't see her, too focused on the buildings, but the reader sees: a quiet observer, recording what the adults miss, seeing what is rather than what was or what could be.

Sophie moved from storefront to storefront, pausing to jot notes. She noted faded paint — sky blue, once cheerful; pale green, now sickly. Rooflines that bowed under the weight of time. Windows that still held a ghost of their former shine. Her fingers brushed carved wood trim hidden beneath layers of flaking paint, ironwork bent but salvageable.

With each step, she breathed in the square — the heat rising from the brick, the dry tang of rust, the bittersweet scent of flowers blooming stubbornly in cracked planters.

And with each step, Marigold settled deeper into her bones. Not just as a place to fix, but as a place that deserved to be fought for.

Cal and the First Collaboration

She found him at the edge of the square, sleeves rolled, sweat darkening his faded work shirt. His tool belt hung heavy at his hip, the worn leather molded to his frame like a second skin. He was crouched over a bench, one leg braced, hammer in hand, driving a stubborn nail into the cracked wood with the kind of care that said he wasn't just fixing furniture — he was fighting back against the square's slow collapse.

"Cal," Sophie called, the word tasting cautious on her tongue.

He straightened, pushing damp hair off his forehead with the back of his hand. His gaze found hers, wary but not hostile — like a man measuring whether to lower the drawbridge or leave it up.

"Figured you'd be off drawing up more plans," he said, not unkindly, just guarded.

"I've got enough plans," she said, taking a step closer. The air smelled of sun-warmed wood and the faint metallic tang of rust. "I want to see the square through your eyes. I want to understand what matters before I get it wrong."

His eyes narrowed slightly, searching her face for cracks. "You serious about that?"

"I wouldn't ask if I wasn't."

Cal exhaled slowly, as if weighing the risk of saying yes.

"Fine," he said at last. "But don't expect me to sugar-coat anything. You wanted the truth — you'll get it."

Side by side, they walked the square, their footsteps echoing off empty storefronts and weathered walls. Cal stopped often, gesturing to cracked facades where vines clawed at flaking paint, to porch posts that leaned like drunks at closing time, to doors warped by years of storms and sun.

"They're stories," he said, voice low, more to himself than to her. "Every nail, every board. You tear them down without understanding them, you don't just lose buildings. You rip out what little's left holding folks here."

He showed her the hardware store his grandfather had opened, later run by his father — shuttered since the recession, its windows cloudy with grime. The bakery that had served three generations of wedding cakes and Sunday donuts, now silent. The church hall with the cracked bell that hadn't rung in years.

Sophie listened, jotting occasional notes, but mostly just absorbing his words, the cadence of them, the care beneath the gruffness.

When they reached the fountain, Cal crouched, running his fingers along a seam in the stone, wiping away dirt to reveal the faint gleam beneath.

"This stone can be saved," he murmured, as if speaking to the fountain itself. "The granite's good. The mortar's shot, but that can be fixed."

Sophie knelt beside him, tracing the edge where his hand had passed. For the first time, they saw the same thing — not just a relic, but something worth saving, worth fighting for.

Their shoulders brushed again — this time without tension, just shared purpose. In that small shared act, the distance between outsider and protector narrowed — just a little, but enough to matter.

A Deeper Threat

They parted with a nod — a fragile truce, sealed not in words but in the quiet understanding of two people who, for a fleeting moment, saw the same future.

Sophie turned, ready to let the weight of that small victory buoy her forward. But then she saw him.

At the far end of the square, near the corner where the old pharmacy's sign hung crooked and rust-streaked, stood a man who didn't belong. His suit was the kind of precise that cost more than most of the town's residents made in a month — dark, tailored sharp at the shoulders, not a crease out of place despite the heat. A tablet rested in one hand, the other tapping the screen as he studied the square like it was a chessboard he'd already won.

His gaze swept the empty shops, the sagging awnings, the fountain's cracked basin. But it wasn't with nostalgia, or even curiosity. It was appraisal. Sophie had seen that look before, in boardrooms and city halls

— the gaze of someone who didn't see a community, only a portfolio waiting to be flipped.

Atlanta. Of course. The word clenched like a fist around her heart.

The man turned slightly, speaking into a headset she hadn't noticed, nodding as if confirming some quiet verdict. A gust of wind lifted his tie, and Sophie felt a chill despite the sun's heat.

Time was slipping through her fingers.

No more talk. No more distance. This has to get real now.

She drew a slow breath, feeling the square beneath her feet — the uneven bricks, the grit of time and neglect. The square wasn't just a place anymore. It was the line she couldn't let them cross.

And somewhere deep inside, determination sparked, fierce and clear.

A Tiny Win

As the sun dipped low, spilling gold and rose across the worn brick of the square, Sophie spotted the teenager from the park still at it — shoulders hunched, plastic bag heavy now with the day's debris. He moved slow but steady, determined in a way that made Sophie pause.

Without a word, she set her bag on the fountain's edge. The soft thunk echoed in the stillness. She rolled up her sleeves, the fabric creased with dust from the day, and bent to join him.

Together they worked — side by side, no introductions, no explanations. Just the quiet rhythm of small tasks: paper lifted from the cracks between bricks, crushed cans clinked into a second bag she pulled from her tote.

The square seemed to exhale as they moved. A breeze stirred the litter they hadn't yet reached, carrying with it the mingled scents of honeysuckle, warm stone, and the faint trace of fried food from a diner that hadn't served a customer all day.

Across the square, Cal leaned against the bed of his truck, arms crossed, watching. Something flickered in his gaze — surprise, maybe respect, though he'd never say so. And maybe — though he wouldn't admit that either — a flicker of something else.

The kind of pretty that crept up on a man — steady, quiet, and impossible to ignore.

The way the evening light caught the loose strands of her hair, the set of her shoulders as she worked, the focus in her face as she gathered the pieces of the square one scrap at a time. She wasn't here to make speeches. She was here to work.

Sophie didn't see him. She didn't look up. Her world had narrowed to the ground beneath her feet, to the act of reclaiming the square one scrap at a time.

When the bags were full, the last rays of sunlight slipping behind the church steeple, Sophie straightened. Her hands were streaked with grime, her back ached from the hours, but there was hope in her chest — small, quiet, but solid.

No speeches. No plans. Just work — the kind Marigold might believe in.

And for the first time that day, Sophie allowed herself a real, unguarded smile.

Chapter 4

Foundations and Fractures

The envelope wasn't just thick — it was *heavy*. Heavy with promise, or perhaps with consequence. Sophie stared at it where it lay on the worn desk in her room at the Marigold House. The morning sun angled through the curtains, casting a stripe of gold across the embossed letterhead.

She hesitated before opening it, letting the weight of the moment settle. She imagined her mother's voice: *"Go on now, Sophie-girl. Rip the bandage off."*

Her fingers broke the seal, unfolding the letter with care, as if roughness might change the words.

Approved

The word seemed to hum off the page.

The preservation-modernization grant. Months of planning, writing, fighting for every comma — and it had paid off.

Sophie crossed to the window, heart racing, and looked down at the square. The fountain caught the light, cracked but still standing. The storefronts leaned against time like weary soldiers.

But the letter's next lines tempered her joy.

"Award contingent upon joint committee leadership and preservation-development partnership at all stages. Milestone reviews to ensure balance of historic

integrity and modern function."

She read it twice, the meaning clear. No lone vision. No clean command. A shared path — with Cal named as co-lead on the committee, whether he liked it or not.

The square seemed to gaze back at her, waiting.

And Sophie whispered, not to the letter, but to herself: "All right, Marigold. Let's see if we can do this together."

The First Site Day

The square buzzed with a different energy that morning — purposeful, cautious, but hopeful. Trucks parked at odd angles. Clipboards clutched in capable hands. Tape measures, chalk lines, and the occasional clang of a hammer testing a beam.

Sophie stood beside Cal as the structural engineer approached — a compact woman with steel-gray hair and eyes that missed nothing. She circled the bakery, running her palm over the crumbling brickwork.

"The outer wall's gone soft in places," she said. "Moisture got in. It's bowing here." She pointed to a hairline crack snaking toward the roofline.

Sophie nodded, jotting notes. "We may need to rebuild the facade, salvage what trim we can."

Cal frowned, stepping closer to the wall. His hand rested against the brick as if he could will it whole.

"It's held this long," he said. "We can brace it. Shore it up from inside. Tearing it down should be the last resort."

Sophie met his gaze. "I'm not looking to tear it down, Cal. But I won't risk someone's safety either."

The engineer cleared her throat gently. "Let's document everything. We can run the load calculations before we make any decisions."

They moved on, the local mason pointing out where old mortar had turned to dust, where stones could be reset rather than replaced. The carpenter — wiry, sunburned, with a cigarette tucked behind one ear —

showed them how some porch beams could be sistered, new wood bolstering the old.

At the fountain, the group paused. The mason crouched, brushing aside dirt to reveal the seam where old granite met a newer patch of cement.

"This base is solid," he said. "You've got something to work with here. It'll take time, but it's worth saving."

Cal shot Sophie a look — not triumphant, not smug, just *solid*, like the stone beneath them.

Sophie returned it, a small smile tugging at the corner of her mouth. "For once, we agree."

And in that moment, the square didn't feel like a battlefield. It felt like common ground.

As the day wore on, the work site slowly quieted — tools packed away, trucks rumbling off down Main Street, voices lowered from discussion to fatigue. But Sophie's mind stayed busy. Every note she'd taken, every compromise reached, every detail debated — all of it pointed to the same truth: the buildings weren't the hardest part of this restoration. The people were.

By late afternoon, word had spread that the grant was real, that changes were coming. And with word came worry — whispered in doorways, traded over shop counters, mulled at kitchen tables.

That's why Sophie had called for the forum. Before the work could move forward, the town needed its say. And she needed to hear it.

A Frayed Public Forum

The town hall smelled of old wood, floor polish, and the sharp tang of nervous energy. Sophie stood near the front, behind a folding table covered with printouts — architectural renderings, budget drafts, timelines. She'd straightened them three times already, trying to steady herself.

The room was packed. Farmers in work boots, retirees in ball caps, young parents with children fidgeting at their sides. The air buzzed with low murmurs — the kind that came before a storm.

Jeanine sat near the middle, sharp-eyed and silent, a yellow legal pad balanced on her lap. Cal leaned against the wall near the side door, arms crossed, watching — always watching.

Sophie cleared her throat, the microphone squealing before settling.

"I appreciate everyone coming tonight," she began, her voice calm, though her pulse raced. "I'm not here to tell Marigold what to be. I'm here because I believe in what it *can* be — with all of you. This grant is a chance to save what matters, to honor what's come before while building a future that can sustain us."

The room stayed quiet a beat too long, then the murmuring rose again.

From the back, Mr. Jasper Calloway stood — a man whose frame had thinned with age but whose voice still boomed with authority.

"We've heard promises before, Ms. Caldwell," he said, cane tapping the floor for emphasis. "Every outsider comes with a map and a mission. And when they leave, we're the ones sweeping up the pieces."

A ripple of agreement — a few heads nodding, a few voices muttering.

Before Sophie could answer, Cal's voice cut through — steady, low, but carrying to every corner.

"She's not like them."

The room turned as one, surprise flickering in the air.

Cal pushed off the wall, stepping forward, the weight of his wordless years lending power to every syllable.

"She didn't come in here trying to buy us out, or sell us off. She's asking to work with us. And we'd be fools not to listen."

Jasper frowned, leaning harder on his cane. "And you're her champion now?"

Cal met his gaze without flinching. "No. I'm Marigold's. That's why I'm here."

Sophie stared at him, stunned silent by the unexpected grace of his defense.

The tension in the room didn't vanish — but it shifted, softened at the edges.

"I don't expect trust overnight," Sophie said quietly. "But I'm here. I'm not leaving when it gets hard. And I'm listening."

No one else rose to challenge her. The meeting dissolved slowly, in small conversations, people lingering longer than they meant to, curious despite themselves.

And as Sophie packed up her papers, Cal lingered at the doorway, his gaze thoughtful, his presence steady — like the square itself, weathered but still standing.

The Personal Cracks Widen

The hall emptied slowly, the last of the voices fading into the night beyond the open doors. The square outside lay bathed in silver moonlight, the fountain casting a long, broken shadow across the bricks.

Sophie stayed behind, gathering the papers she'd spread across the table — but her hands moved on their own, her mind replaying every word, every doubt she'd heard tonight.

She didn't notice Cal until the chair beside her scraped softly against the worn floorboards.

"You handled them better than I would've," he said, his voice quieter than before — no edge now, just honesty.

Sophie sank into the chair, exhaustion catching up with her. "Didn't feel like I handled anything. I felt like I was patching a dam with my bare hands."

Cal gave a soft huff of breath — not quite a laugh, not quite sympathy. "That's Marigold for you."

For a long moment, they sat in the quiet. The kind of quiet that comes when people stop performing, stop defending, and just *are*.

Sophie stared down at her notes, then spoke without looking at him.

"My mother stood in this hall once, too. Tried to start a cooperative — get folks to pool their savings, back each other's businesses. Said if we didn't invest in ourselves, no one else would."

Her voice faltered, but she forced herself on. "No one backed her. They smiled, said nice words, and let it die. She never said it broke her heart, but I saw it in her face every day after. And when we left… I think part of her stayed here, with everything she tried to save."

Cal's hands folded on the table, knuckles scarred and strong, fingers stained with years of work.

"I know that feeling," he said after a long pause. His voice was low, almost rough. "Every time I fix a roof, patch a porch, I wonder if it's enough. If I'm just biding time until this place gives up. I think about Emma. I've tried to keep things simple for her. But simple's not enough anymore, is it? I'm scared I'm holding her in a place that won't be hers much longer."

The name caught Sophie, soft and unexpected. Emma. His daughter, she assumed — but how could she be sure? A wife? A sister? A family she'd never imagined? The question rose, then settled, unanswered. This wasn't the moment to ask. But the wondering stayed with her, quiet as the night.

Then their eyes met — stripped of pretense, of old fights and fresh arguments.

"We're both trying to keep promises," Sophie said softly.

"Yeah," Cal agreed, voice so quiet it was almost a whisper. "And scared of breaking them."

They sat that way, not needing more words, as the night held them in its gentle hush — two people, side by side, feeling the cracks and realizing maybe, just maybe, they could help hold each other up.

An Act of Grace

The next afternoon, the square glowed under a mild sun, softened by a high veil of clouds. The heat of the day held back for once, and a breeze carried the sweet scent of clover and the faintest trace of fresh bread from somewhere Sophie couldn't place.

She was kneeling near the fountain, sketching lines in her notebook, trying to work out how to balance the old stone with the new piping the mason had recommended. The edges of her pages curled in the breeze, and she pressed them flat, focused, but weary — her mind as full of fractures as the square itself.

"Hi."

The voice was quiet, but clear. Sophie looked up.

Emma stood a few feet away, sketchbook under one arm, a plate balanced carefully in her hands. Two slices of pound cake, pale gold and dusted with sugar, gleamed in the soft light.

"I didn't mean to interrupt," Emma added, cheeks pink. She hesitated, then added, "I'm Emma, by the way."

Sophie smiled, genuinely touched. "You're not interrupting at all."

The name echoed in Sophie's mind — *Emma*. So this was the Emma Cal had spoken of. His daughter. The wondering she'd carried the night before settled quietly into certainty.

Emma stepped closer, setting the plate on the edge of the fountain. She glanced down at Sophie's notes, curiosity flickering in her gaze.

"My mom used to bake that for our park picnics... before she got sick," Emma said, almost shyly. "We're having one now, over at the park. I thought maybe you'd want to come. Or just… have some cake."

Sophie's throat tightened. The gesture was simple, but it felt like the first real invitation she'd been offered here — unprompted, unearned, and all the more precious for it.

"I'd like that," Sophie said softly.

Emma's smile brightened, small but true. "Okay. I'll tell Dad."

Sophie hesitated. "Emma? Thank you."

The girl shrugged with the casual grace of someone who didn't think kindness was a big deal. "Everyone's got to eat," she said, and turned, jogging back across the square toward the cluster of families near the park — blankets spread, coolers open, the low hum of laughter filling the air.

Sophie watched her go, the plate of cake warm against her palm. She glanced across the square and saw Cal, standing beneath a tree, arms crossed as always. But his gaze wasn't hard this time. When their eyes met, he gave a small, almost imperceptible nod.

And in that moment, Sophie felt something shift — not a collapse of walls, but a door cracked open.

She picked up the plate, took a bite, and let the sweetness steady her.

Foreshadowing Trouble

Evening crept in gently, washing the square in soft lavender and gold. The picnic had begun to wind down — blankets folded, coolers snapped shut, the low hum of conversation turning toward goodbyes. The air smelled of grass and cooling earth, touched with the sweetness of Emma's cake still lingering on Sophie's tongue.

For a moment, Sophie let herself breathe. The square seemed almost peaceful — as if, for once, it could be what she imagined: a place of belonging, of future.

But then, from the far end of the square, she noticed him.

A man in a pale suit, sharp as glass, shoes polished to a mirror shine. He moved with unhurried confidence, tablet tucked under one arm, pausing now and then to take photos, to trace the line of a roof with his gaze as if measuring its worth in dollars and cents rather than memory. It was the same man — the Atlanta developer she'd seen once before, sharp and silent, studying the square like a chessboard. Only now, his moves were starting.

Sophie's stomach knotted.

He stopped at the antique shop, where Mrs. Calder was sweeping her stoop. The man's smile was practiced, precise. He offered a card, spoke words Sophie couldn't hear but could easily imagine — promises wrapped in polish, numbers whispered like temptation.

Mrs. Calder hesitated, fingers brushing the edge of the card before she accepted it, her eyes flicking toward Sophie with something between apology and resignation.

The man moved on, his stride easy, his focus sharp. He circled the square as if drawing invisible lines on a map only he could see.

Sophie stayed where she was, heart pounding, watching as he disappeared down Main Street, his figure swallowed by the dusk.

The breeze stirred her papers on the fountain's edge, scattering a few toward the bricks. Sophie gathered them with trembling hands, but it wasn't the papers she was afraid of losing.

The square wasn't theirs alone to save anymore.

If she and Cal didn't act — if they didn't *earn* this town's trust, fast — someone else would take it, reshape it, sell it off piece by piece.

Sophie straightened, her resolve settling hard as stone.

No more talk. No more distance. This has to get real.

And as night deepened around her, the square felt less like a dream waiting to be restored, and more like common ground turning into a battleground — one they'd have to defend together.

Chapter 5

Sparks and Setbacks

The town square lay hushed under the cover of night, its empty windows reflecting moonlight like watchful eyes. Inside the old hardware store—temporary headquarters for the restoration project—Sophie and Cal sat hunched over a makeshift worktable. The space smelled of sawdust, ink, and coffee that had long since gone cold.

Blueprints covered every surface, curling at the edges, smudged where fingers traced the lines too many times. A single lamp cast a soft pool of light, leaving the corners of the room in shadow.

Sophie pushed a pencil behind her ear, frustration threading through her voice. "If we shift the fountain plumbing here"—she tapped the page—"we can preserve the stonework and meet code. But we'll need custom fittings. Two weeks' delay, minimum."

Cal rubbed the back of his neck, fatigue making his features sharper, more vulnerable. "And if we don't? We tear out the base and lose the original stone."

Their eyes met across the table — both knowing neither option felt right.

Sophie exhaled, leaning back. "I'm sorry. I'm trying not to bulldoze your history."

Cal's mouth twitched — the ghost of a smile. "You're not bulldozing anything. You care too much — that's half the problem."

Silence settled, companionable and taut at once. Cal reached for the pencil Sophie had set down. Their fingers brushed — warm skin against warm skin, brief but enough to send a flicker through both of them.

Sophie froze. The contact was nothing. Everything.

A memory surged, unbidden — her mother's hand on hers, steadying her the night before they left Marigold. *"You'll have to build your own strength, Sophie-girl. Brick by brick. And it'll scare you sometimes — that's how you'll know it matters."*

Her throat tightened. *It matters.*

She looked away first, heart thudding louder than seemed fair. "Coffee?"

"God, yes," Cal said, voice low, roughened by more than exhaustion.

She poured from the thermos, handing him a mug. His fingers closed over hers for a heartbeat longer than necessary.

"Thanks," he said.

"For the coffee or the company?"

His eyes held hers, the hint of challenge softened now by something else. "Both."

They sipped in the quiet, the night stretching out around them, filled with more than blueprints and deadlines.

Emma's Quiet Plea

The next afternoon, Marigold's small library smelled of sun-warmed wood, old paper, and lemon polish. Dust motes danced in the light streaming through tall windows, and the soft rustle of pages turning echoed in the hush.

Sophie stood at the local history shelves, fingertip tracing faded labels, seeking clues about the square's past. Her notebook was already half-filled with sketches and questions.

"Hi," came a voice, soft but clear.

Sophie turned. Emma stood a few feet away, notebook hugged to her chest, hair tucked behind one ear. She looked as if she'd almost lost her nerve at the last second.

Sophie smiled, gentle. "Hey there."

Emma took a breath, glanced at her father where he sat across the room leafing through a hardware manual — watching, but pretending not to.

"I was wondering…" Emma hesitated, cheeks coloring. "If you'd maybe help me? For school. We're supposed to do a project about Marigold's history. The square, the fountain — stuff like that."

Sophie blinked, then softened. *A bridge,* she thought. Emma was offering a bridge, whether she realized it or not.

"I'd love to help," Sophie said, kneeling to be eye-level. "Tell me what you've got so far."

Emma opened her notebook, revealing delicate sketches of the fountain, the old movie theater, the big oak tree on Main. Notes in careful handwriting filled the margins.

Sophie studied the pages, impressed. "You're good at this. Really good."

Emma ducked her head, pleased. "Thanks. I want it to be… right. Not just for school. For Dad." Sophie's heart tugged. "Then let's make it right."

They sat cross-legged on the worn carpet between the shelves, books and notes spread between them. Sophie shared what she'd learned — how the fountain's original stone had been quarried nearby, how the movie house once hosted traveling vaudeville shows.

Emma listened intently, asking thoughtful questions, adding to her notes.

And across the room, Cal glanced up from his manual. He watched them a moment — Sophie and Emma, heads bent close over the pages, laughter slipping between their words — and something in his gaze softened, wary walls cracking just a little more.

When they finished, Emma closed her notebook, satisfied.

"Thank you," she said.

Sophie smiled. "Anytime."

Emma hesitated, then said shyly, "You should come by after school sometime. We could work on it more. Or… just hang out."

Sophie's chest ached in the best way. "I'd like that."

Emma beamed, and Sophie watched as she skipped back to Cal, who stood with that quiet pride only a father could wear — his hand lingering like he didn't want to let go.

And for the first time, Sophie felt she might be finding her place not just in the square, but in the fabric of this town.

The Rival Developer Makes a Move

The mood in the square shifted like the wind — subtle at first, then impossible to ignore.

It started with whispers. Sophie heard them in the café line, on the sidewalk outside the library, from Jeanine behind the counter at the bookstore.

"Did you hear? Old Man Greeley's shop — under contract."

"McDougal's feed store too. Full price, no contingencies."

"Out-of-towners. Big offer. Quick close."

Sophie's stomach sank.

By noon, the whispers had become reality. Cal found her near the fountain, papers under one arm, face tight with frustration.

"We've got a problem," he said, without preamble.

Sophie braced herself. "What is it?"

Cal held up a flyer — glossy, polished, the kind that spoke of money to burn.

"Marigold Rising — A Modern Vision for a Historic Town."

It bore the sleek logo of the Atlanta developer. Beneath it, promises: luxury lofts, curated shopping experiences, and a square reimagined for tomorrow's lifestyle. Renderings showed a clean, sterile vision — slick brick facades, polished steel signage, streetlamps that looked like they belonged in a theme park.

Sophie scanned it, heart pounding.

"They're buying up key properties," Cal said, voice low and taut. "Greeley's, McDougal's, maybe even the old mercantile — the one we pegged as the cornerstone of the plan."

"That building anchors the whole design," Sophie said, the words tight in her throat. "If they get it, we lose the chance to keep the square's integrity."

Cal's jaw worked, the muscle tight at his temple. "They're offering cash, no strings, more than the buildings are worth. Folks are tempted. Hell, I don't blame them — they're tired, Sophie. Tired of promises. Tired of waiting."

The square around them felt smaller, as if the buildings' walls were closing in, threatening to suffocate the vision they'd barely begun to build.

Sophie turned, scanning the storefronts — familiar now, dear in their imperfection. She spotted Mrs. Calder in the doorway of her antique shop, the glossy flyer folded in one hand, eyes troubled. The rival's plan was taking root.

And worse — Sophie felt the tension spark between herself and Cal.

"You knew they'd come back," Cal said, not accusing, but close. "You knew they'd circle. And now they're picking us apart one deed at a time."

"We can still stop this," Sophie said, trying to steady the moment. "If we move fast. If we pull the town together."

Cal shook his head, anger and fear battling behind his eyes. "The town's fractured, Sophie. And this — this might be what breaks it for good."

Sophie felt the weight of it — the grant, the plans, the fragile trust, all on the brink.

And in that moment, she knew: this was the real fight.

Not just blueprints and bricks.

But hearts.

And hope.

A Heated Argument

The storm broke on the square's edge.

They hadn't meant to argue, not here, not now. But as the last of the sunlight faded and the rival developer's flyers littered the sidewalks like autumn leaves, Sophie and Cal found themselves face to face — no more polite distance, no more holding back.

"I can't believe you didn't see this coming," Cal said, his voice low but sharp. "You come in here with your plans and your grants and your promises, but you didn't think about how vulnerable we are — how desperate folks would be to take the first real offer that came their way."

Sophie felt the sting of his words — because they weren't entirely unfair. But the heat rising in her chest demanded its say.

"I *did* think about it," she shot back. "I think about it every damn day. But I'm not the one who let the square fall apart in the first place. You've been here, Cal — *you* saw it coming long before I ever stepped off that train. Don't put this all on me."

His eyes flashed, his stance tightening as if bracing against a wind. "I stayed, Sophie. I did what I could. You think I haven't patched roofs, fixed porches, tried to keep this place breathing? You think it's easy watching it die one cracked brick at a time?"

Her voice rose, the frustration, fear, and sheer fatigue spilling out. "And you think it's easy trying to save a place that fights you every step of the way? I'm doing everything I can — but you're so scared of change you can't see I'm *on your side.*"

"On my side?" Cal laughed — a bitter sound, not cruel but wounded. "You're on the side of whatever plan keeps you from failing. And maybe you do care — I'm not saying you don't — but you don't know what it's like to *live* with the weight of this place every day. You don't wake up wondering if today's the day it's too far gone to fix."

The words cut deeper than he meant. Sophie flinched, but stood her ground.

"You're right," she said, her voice quieter now, raw around the edges. "I don't live with that weight — not like you do. But don't you dare tell me I don't *feel* it. Don't you dare stand there and act like I don't want this as much as you do. Because I do. Maybe more. Because I made a promise to a dying woman, and I don't intend to break it."

For a heartbeat, Cal said nothing. The anger ebbed, leaving behind the ache beneath — the shared fear, the shared longing to get it right.

"I don't want to fight you," he said at last, the words heavy with truth.

"Neither do I," Sophie whispered.

But they had — and both knew they weren't done yet.

The square around them seemed to hold its breath, the first stars blinking awake overhead as if waiting to see what came next.

And in the charged stillness, both realized: this wasn't just about blueprints and buildings anymore. It was about movement — of trust, of hearts, of everything between what was and what might still be.

The Compromise Plan

Night settled fully over Marigold, the square bathed in the soft glow of lamplight, the sharp edges of their argument still lingering in the air. Sophie and Cal stood apart at first, both trying to cool the fire inside.

Sophie moved to the fountain, palms braced against the cold stone, breathing deep. The air smelled of damp brick, honeysuckle, and the faintest trace of woodsmoke from some distant chimney. *There has to be a way,* she told herself. *There always is.*

Behind her, Cal paced, boots scuffing against the uneven bricks. His fists clenched and unclenched at his sides, frustration giving way to thought. He hated how right she'd been — hated more that he'd let his fear turn on the one person fighting beside him.

Finally, Sophie turned, voice low but steady. "I've been thinking. The big developers have money — more than we can match. But we have something they don't."

Cal stopped pacing, wary but listening. "What's that?"

Sophie stepped closer, eyes clear now, focused. "People who care about this place. Not just the ones living here now — but the ones who left, the ones who have family buried in the cemetery, who still call it home even from a thousand miles away. We tap into that. We offer a way for them to be part of saving it."

Cal frowned, trying to keep up. "You're talking donations?"

"Bigger than that. Historical bonds, community co-ops, investment trusts—ways for people with roots in Marigold to hold a stake in its future. We make saving this town something they can own — literally."

Cal stared at her, a dozen emotions crossing his face — skepticism, surprise, and, finally, something that looked like hope.

"You really think people would go for it?"

"I think they'll go for *us*, if they believe we mean it. If they see we're not just fighting each other, but fighting *for* something together."

The quiet between them shifted — less charged now, more aligned.

Cal rubbed a hand over his face, weariness giving way to resolve. "It's a hell of a long shot."

Sophie smiled, the first real smile since their fight. "Marigold's always been worth a long shot."

He nodded slowly. "Okay. Let's do it. Let's give them something real to believe in."

And just like that, they turned back to the work — not because the tension was gone, but because the fight was bigger than either of them.

The Dance

The Harvest Festival filled the square with light and life. Strings of bulbs looped from lamppost to lamppost, casting soft halos over the crowd.

The music of a small local band rose and fell, sweet with fiddle and guitar, threading through the night like a promise.

Sophie stood by the fountain, the cool stone at her back, watching the town pulse around her. Children darted past, faces sticky with caramel and cider. Neighbors clustered at booths, voices warm with the comfort of shared history. The scent of woodsmoke, kettle corn, and spiced apples filled the air, and for the first time since arriving, Sophie felt Marigold's heart beating strong beneath her feet.

Then she felt it — that quiet pull.

Cal, across the square, his gaze steady as it found hers. He'd been helping set up tables, moving hay bales for makeshift seating, but now he stood still, as if the world had narrowed to this: her.

She didn't look away. A small, uncertain smile curved her lips — the kind of smile that invited rather than promised.

Jeanine appeared at her side, breathless from laughter, a paper plate balanced in one hand. "That boy's trying to work up the nerve, you know," she said with a wink. "Best not make him sweat too long."

Before Sophie could answer, Cal crossed the distance, the crowd parting for him as if they felt the weight of the moment too. He stopped in front of her, hesitated, then held out his hand.

"One dance," he said, low enough that only she could hear.

His palm was calloused, warm, waiting.

Sophie hesitated, her heart thudding, knowing that taking his hand meant more than just a turn on the bricks. It meant stepping into whatever this was between them — the push and pull, the promise and peril of it.

She placed her hand in his, and the world softened at the edges.

The music shifted — a waltz, gentle and slow, old as the square itself. Cal's arm settled at her waist, his other hand clasping hers, and they began to move, tentative at first, then finding the rhythm together.

Sophie's dress brushed against the worn bricks as they turned, the lights glinting off the silver at her ears, the night air cool against the heat rising between them.

"You're lighter on your feet than I expected," she said, a smile tugging at her mouth.

Cal's eyes crinkled at the corners. "And you're braver than you let on."

Around them, townsfolk watched — not with suspicion, but with something closer to wonder. Mrs. Clemens murmured to Jeanine, "Well, I'll be." The mayor's wife nudged her husband, both of them smiling. Even the teenagers stopped their horsing around for a beat, sensing the shift in the square's mood.

As they danced, Sophie felt the music seep into her bones, felt the tension of weeks uncoil. The world — the grants, the rival developers, the fractures — faded, leaving only this: the weight of his hand, the steady sound of his breathing, the quiet possibility of two people trying to move as one.

The song ended, but they lingered, hands still joined, the space between them charged with everything unsaid.

"Thank you," Sophie said, voice soft.

Cal's thumb brushed her knuckles before letting go. "Anytime," he said, and meant it.

And as they stepped apart, the square seemed changed — as if, in that dance, something had been set in motion that no rival plan could stop.

Cal's Reckoning

Later that night, long after the music faded and the last strings of lights blinked out, Cal stood alone on his porch, the square quiet again, the stars sharp above the rooftops. The cool air smelled of woodsmoke and the sweet remains of festival cider spilled on the bricks.

He braced his hands on the railing, the rough wood familiar beneath his palms. His heart still beat too fast — not from the dance itself, but from what it stirred.

He hadn't planned to ask her. God knew, he'd fought against the impulse. But when Sophie smiled across the square, when her eyes met his with that open, steady kind of courage — something in him had moved before his mind could stop it.

And now here he was, feeling like a man torn in two.

He thought of Lena — his wife, gone six years now. The way she'd laughed when he first tried to teach her to dance on this very porch. The way she'd smelled of lilac and sawdust after helping him in the shop. The way she'd loved Marigold — fiercely, stubbornly, the same way he did.

Gone six years now. And yet, some nights, he swore he could hear her voice in the breeze. *"Don't let this place die, Cal. Promise me."*

He had. He always would.

But tonight, as Sophie's hand fit in his, as they'd moved together beneath the lights, he'd felt the weight of that promise shift. Not lessen — never that. But change. Because for the first time since Lena's passing, he'd wondered what it might feel like not to carry it alone.

And that terrified him.

He stared out at the square, quiet now, but still holding the echo of their waltz. The town watched, he knew. They'd seen the dance. They'd seen him falter — and maybe, just maybe, begin again.

Am I betraying her? The question came unbidden, sharp as any blade. His throat tightened against it.

But another voice rose in him, quieter, steadier — maybe Lena's, maybe his own. *You're not betraying her. You're keeping the promise. And maybe that means letting someone stand with you.*

Cal closed his eyes, drew a long breath, and let it out slow. The square waited, the future waited. And whatever came next — he'd face it. One step at a time.

Chapter 6

Crossing the Threshold

It began with sirens, wailing down Main Street before the sun had cleared the rooftops.

Sophie sat alone in the inn's parlor, cold coffee in hand, the remnants of sleep clinging to her like fog.

The square outside was quiet, touched with early light — shop windows blinking awake, a dog nosing the sidewalk, the scent of baking bread drifting from somewhere she couldn't place.

Then Mrs. Clemens appeared in the doorway, apron askew, eyes wide with alarm.

"They've done it," she said, voice tight. "They filed those demolition papers. It's in the Gazette."

She thrust the morning paper toward Sophie. Sophie's stomach sank before she even unfolded it.

HISTORIC POST OFFICE FACES DEMOLITION

Developer Fast-Tracks Permits in 72-Hour Move

A glossy rendering sprawled across the bottom half of the page — all glass angles and polished stone, towering over the square like a threat.

Sophie was out the door before she'd even registered grabbing her bag.

By the time she reached the square, a knot of townspeople had gathered in front of the old post office. The building, sun-washed and crumbling at the edges, stood like a sentinel at the corner of Main and Willow — the place where generations had mailed letters, lined up for stamps, traded gossip in the echoing lobby.

A garish neon-orange placard was slapped to the door:

NOTICE OF DEMOLITION

Property of Marigold Revitalization Partners, LLC.

Demolition scheduled within 72 hours.

The crowd was growing — shop owners, students late for school, farmers in from the fields.

"They can't do this," Jeanine Marks said, pushing to the front. Her voice cracked with fury. "That building's our history. Our soul."

"This ain't revitalization," muttered old Mr. Reed, arms folded tight. "This is erasure."

Councilwoman Hester Boyd tried to raise her hands for calm, but her voice wobbled. "Let's not rush to judgment. The zoning approvals go way back. It's... complicated."

"That's a convenient word for betrayal," Jeanine snapped.

Sophie scanned the faces — fear, grief, fury. She felt it, too. The weight of failure already pressing at her ribs.

Then she spotted him.

Cal stood apart at first, his stance rigid, fists clenched at his sides. His gaze was fixed on the post office, as if sheer will could hold back the wrecking ball. The sun caught the lines of strain in his face.

When he turned and met Sophie's eyes, the air between them seemed to tighten.

"You said you had a plan," he said, voice low, barely audible above the crowd's rising clamor. "Well? What now, Caldwell?"

It wasn't taunt or scorn — it was a plea masked as a challenge.

Sophie's mind raced. *Think. There's always a way. There's always leverage.*

And even as the square buzzed with anger and despair, Sophie felt resolve take root. She could not — would not — let this be how Marigold fell.

Sophie Steps Up

The crowd's voices rose and fell in waves — anger, confusion, helplessness. A man near the fountain kicked at a loose brick, sending it skittering across the square. Mrs. Clemens stood stiff-backed, arms folded, as if holding herself together against the tide.

Sophie's mind raced. *There's a way. There has to be.*

She felt Cal's gaze — steady, expectant, as if this was the moment that would prove what kind of person she really was.

Her pulse hammered. She pulled out her phone, fingers flying as she scrolled to a contact she hadn't called in over a year: Elena Torres, now a senior advocate at the State Heritage Council, a woman Sophie had once helped win a preservation grant against long odds.

The first ring felt like an eternity. Then:

"Elena Torres."

"Elena, it's Sophie Caldwell. We worked together on the Sandridge Depot project? I need help. Now."

Her voice shook, but the words were clear. Sophie stepped away from the crowd, heart pounding, shielding the phone with one hand against the rising wind.

"Elena, there's a historic post office about to be torn down. Permits pushed through by an out-of-town developer. We have community support. A plan in motion. I need an injunction — temporary protection, heritage status pending — anything that'll buy us time."

Elena didn't hesitate. "Get me affidavits. A copy of the town's preservation filings. Photos. Letters from residents if you can. I'll call the district judge's clerk and see what I can do from this end. But we have to move fast."

"I'm on it," Sophie said. She ended the call, drew a deep breath, and turned back to face the crowd.

They were watching now — every face. Skeptical, yes, but waiting.

"I'm filing for an injunction today," Sophie said, her voice carrying across the square. "It won't stop the developer forever, but it will give us time — time to fight this the right way, time to show what Marigold stands for."

A beat of stunned silence. Then Jeanine stepped forward, her smile small but fierce.

"Well," she said, voice ringing clear, "it's about time somebody did."

Someone clapped — tentative at first, then stronger. The sound spread, hands joining in, a rough rhythm of approval that filled the square.

Cal moved closer, close enough that Sophie could see the tight line of his mouth ease just a little.

"You really can do that?" he asked, voice low enough for only her.

"I can try," Sophie said. "It's all I've got."

Cal nodded, something new in his eyes — not just respect, but relief. "Then you're not alone in it. Not anymore."

And as Sophie began gathering names, snapping photos, and coordinating statements, Cal was there beside her, lending his voice to hers.

For the first time, it felt like they were fighting the same fight.

The Plan That Could Save It All

The square was nearly empty by nightfall, the tension of the day clinging to the bricks like humidity that wouldn't lift. The injunction had bought them time — barely — but time wasn't a solution. It was a window. And windows closed.

Sophie stood by the fountain, papers in hand, but seeing none of them. The lamp above hummed softly, casting a circle of pale gold around her. Across the square, the faint glow from Cal's workshop spilled onto the sidewalk.

For a moment, she considered retreating — calling it a night, letting exhaustion win. But the image of that glossy rendering from the paper burned behind her eyes. Glass and steel where memory should be. No.

She crossed the square, pushed open the workshop door.

Cal looked up from his workbench, surprise flickering across his face. His sleeves were rolled, hands streaked with grease and sawdust, a pencil tucked behind one ear.

"I didn't think you'd still be at it," she said quietly.

He half-smiled. "Didn't think you would either."

For a heartbeat, they simply stood in the shared quiet, the smell of cedar and machine oil grounding them.

Sophie exhaled. "We can't just stall them. We have to outthink them. Outbuild them. I have ideas, but—"

Cal set down his tools, wiping his hands on a rag. "But?"

"But I can't do this without you."

The admission hung between them.

Cal studied her face, and something in him shifted. "Okay," he said. "Let's figure it out."

They spread plans across the workbench — maps, renderings, napkin sketches. Ideas tumbled out: restored façades that honored the town's past, shared green spaces where kids could play and neighbors could gather, micro-grants for local businesses, sustainable materials sourced nearby.

Cal's reservations softened as he saw the respect in her plans — not for profit, but for place.

He pointed at a sketch. "That alley — what if it became a pedestrian lane? Market stalls, maybe? Keep it ours."

Sophie lit up. "Yes. And the old service yard behind the café — what if we turned it into a pocket garden? Native plants, benches. A space that belongs to everyone."

Their voices overlapped now, the room filling with energy as ideas flowed. They debated rooflines, materials — what could be salvaged, what could be reimagined.

Hours passed unnoticed, the night deepening outside. The square, battered and beautiful, seemed to lean in, listening.

Finally, they stood back, looking at the rough plan they'd built together — imperfect, but theirs.

"We could do this," Cal said, wonder slowly overtaking his doubt.

"Really build something that lasts."

Sophie smiled, tired but hopeful. "We can. We have to."

And for the first time, the future felt closer than the threat.

Emma's Role Grows

The day after the injunction was filed, the square felt different. Not whole — not by a long shot — but no longer helpless. Sophie walked its worn brick paths in the early light, checking in on the posters Jeanine had helped pin up, answering quiet questions from shopkeepers, feeling the shift in the air.

At the library steps, she paused. The building was small, no grand columns or marble floors — just red brick, white trim, and an air of quiet stubbornness that suited Marigold.

"Sophie!"

She turned at the sound of her name. Emma Bennett trotted down the steps, sketchbook hugged to her chest, face flushed from the cold.

"Hi," Sophie said, surprised but smiling. "What's up?"

Emma hesitated, glancing back at the library as if making sure no one else could hear.

"I heard what you did," she said in a rush. "The town's talking about it. About you."

Sophie tried to brush it off. "We bought some time. That's all."

Emma shook her head, eyes bright. "It's more than that. And I was wondering... could you help me? I mean, not for you — for school. We're doing local history projects. I wanted to do mine on the square. On the post office. Before it's too late."

The words hit Sophie like a soft blow. *Before it's too late.*

"Of course," she said, voice gentler now. "I'd be honored to help."

Emma's smile widened, the shyness falling away. She opened her sketchbook to a page crowded with careful pencil lines — the post office's façade, drawn with a precision that made Sophie's throat ache.

"I want to get it right," Emma said. "Not just what it looks like.

What it meant."

Sophie crouched beside her, studying the drawing. "You already are. That's beautiful."

They sat on the steps together, heads bent over the sketchbook as Emma pointed out details: the crack in the stone arch, the faded sign, the old flag bracket no one had bothered to remove.

"Tell me everything you know about it," Emma said. "What it was like before."

And Sophie did. She shared memories — how she and her mother would stop there on Saturday mornings, mailing birthday cards, picking up catalog orders. How her father once brought her there to buy commemorative stamps, letting her choose the sheet with bright flowers and famous faces.

Emma listened, rapt, her pencil moving as Sophie spoke.

As the morning wore on, other kids drifted over, curious. Soon a small knot of them sat cross-legged on the library lawn, sketching, scribbling notes, asking questions.

And in that moment, Sophie realized something Cal had always known — Marigold's future wasn't just in saving buildings. It was in teaching the next generation to care about what they inherited.

Later, as Sophie gathered her things to leave, Emma caught her hand.

"Thank you," she said quietly. "For helping. And for trying."

Across the square, Cal watched — unseen by Sophie. He saw his daughter's easy warmth with this woman who had once been a stranger, and something in him softened, the edges of his resistance worn down by hope.

A Near Kiss

The night air outside Cal's workshop was cool and sweet, tinged with sawdust and honeysuckle. The square lay hushed, bathed in silver by the rising moon. It had been hours since they'd first spread the plans across his battered workbench — hours of sketching, debating, redrawing, building a vision that felt more real with every line.

Now, Sophie stood at the open door, stretching her arms, her shoulders aching with exhaustion and exhilaration both.

"I should go," she said softly, glancing at her watch though she couldn't remember when she last cared about the time.

Cal leaned against the doorway, arms folded, watching her in the half-light. His hair was damp at the temples, shirt sleeves rolled, hands stained with graphite.

"Long night," he said.

"The best kind," Sophie replied, surprising herself.

They stood there, the square spread before them like a promise half-kept. The plans they'd sketched lay on the workbench inside, but it was what lay between them now that hummed with possibility.

Cal cleared his throat, suddenly aware of how close they stood, how the lamplight softened the edge of her features.

"I'll walk you," he said, voice low.

"You don't have to," Sophie replied — but she didn't stop him when he fell into step beside her.

They crossed the square slowly, their footfalls muffled against the worn bricks. The cracked, dry fountain glowed pale beneath the moon. Just beyond, the inn's windows glimmered faintly, a beacon at the edge of the quiet night.

They paused. The night wrapped around them, quiet and intimate.

Sophie fumbled, then stopped, looking up at him. His face was shadowed, unreadable, but his gaze didn't waver.

"Thank you," she said. The words felt heavier than they should have. "For tonight. For trusting me — even just a little."

Cal hesitated, then took a small step closer, drawn in despite himself.

"I didn't want to trust again," he admitted, voice rough. "But I do. And that scares the hell out of me."

Sophie's breath caught. She could feel the heat of him now, the tension strung tight between them. A hand lifted — his — as if to brush a strand of hair from her face, but it stopped halfway, fingers curling in on themselves.

Their eyes met, and for a heartbeat the world narrowed to that space between them — charged, fragile, waiting.

She tilted her head, just slightly. He leaned in, just enough that she could feel the promise of his warmth.

And then —

Cal drew back, breath unsteady. "I can't. Not tonight."

Sophie swallowed hard, nodding though disappointment flickered through her. "I understand."

He managed a ghost of a smile, filled with regret and longing both.

"I want to do this right," he said simply.

And somehow, that meant more than any kiss would have.

"Good night, Cal."

"Night, Sophie."

A Setback

The morning after the long night at Cal's workshop dawned hazy and brittle, as if the world itself were holding its breath. Sophie arrived at the square early, hopeful and bone-tired, the smell of coffee from a nearby shop barely cutting through her fatigue.

She carried their new plan — the one they'd drawn together, piece by hopeful piece — and felt, for the first time, like the tide was turning.

Until she saw Jeanine waiting by the fountain, lips pressed tight, newspaper folded under one arm like a weapon.

"They moved," Jeanine said without preamble, holding out the paper. "Late last night. Before your ink was dry."

Sophie took it, heart sinking.

DEVELOPERS OFFER RECORD BUYOUTS

Several Property Owners Agree to Sell

The words blurred for a moment as Sophie tried to steady herself. Below the headline was a photo: a stranger's handshake with a local shopkeeper, smiles that didn't reach their eyes.

Jeanine's voice was soft now, but no less fierce. "They're dangling checks too big to refuse. Folks who swore they'd never sell — they're signing, Sophie. Because they're scared. Because they're tired. Because hope don't pay the mortgage."

Sophie folded the paper, hands shaking slightly. She scanned the square, and sure enough, she spotted the changes: a developer's glossy sign in the window of the old hardware store. A "sale pending" placard taped to the door of the bakery where Cal had taken Emma for cookies when she was small. The square that had felt, just last night, like it might belong to them again — it seemed to slip further away with every heartbeat.

A truck door slammed, and Cal appeared from across the street, strides long and determined.

"I heard," he said, not bothering to hide the bitterness in his voice.

"I didn't see it coming," Sophie admitted, the weight of it heavy on her chest.

Cal didn't answer right away. He raked a hand through his hair, gaze sweeping the square as if trying to memorize it before it changed forever.

"They're buying up the bones before we can breathe life back into them," he said quietly.

"They're trying to break us before we can even fight," Sophie added.

Cal looked at her then — really looked — and something passed between them: a shared anger, a shared grief, and beneath it, a shared determination.

"We're not done," Sophie said, more to herself than him.

"No," Cal agreed. "We're not."

But as they stood there, the square felt like contested ground — and the cost of losing had never been clearer.

Chapter 7

Beneath the Surface

The town hall was standing-room only, the air thick with anticipation and the scent of coffee, worn wood, and nervous sweat. Folding chairs scraped against the scarred floor as neighbors squeezed in, old rivalries and fragile hopes packed shoulder to shoulder.

Sophie stood near the front, laptop closed, notes folded neatly — for once, words on paper felt like armor she didn't need. Beside her, Cal looked as tense as she'd ever seen him, arms crossed, gaze sweeping the room like he was counting hearts and doubters alike.

Hester Boyd banged the gavel gently. "Let's come to order. Tonight, we'll hear from both parties regarding proposals for the square's future."

Sophie drew a breath and stepped forward.

"Thank you for being here. I know you're tired — of meetings, of promises, of fights that seem to go nowhere. But tonight isn't about speeches. It's about choosing what kind of town we want Marigold to be for the next generation."

She clicked the remote. The screen behind her flickered to life — renderings of their joint plan: the restored fountain, small business fronts repainted and repaired, shared green spaces edged with native blooms, a playground shaded by the old oaks.

"Our proposal isn't perfect," Sophie said. "But it's ours. Built with your input, designed to preserve what matters while making room for what's needed. We want to work with you — not over you."

A murmur rippled through the crowd. Some faces softened; others stayed stony.

Then the rival developer's representative took the floor. He was slick in a tailored suit, hair slicked back, smile polished to a high shine. His voice was smooth as marble.

"Ladies and gentlemen, we respect Ms. Caldwell's passion. Truly. But passion doesn't pay bills or fix leaky roofs. Our plan brings jobs, tax relief, modern amenities. We're ready to invest *now*. No delays, no risky co-ops or untested ideas. Just results."

He gestured to his team — sharp suits, glossy pamphlets — and clicked his own slides: sleek glass storefronts, a boutique hotel, promises of prosperity without the hard questions of how.

"I'm not saying don't dream," he said with practiced charm. "I'm saying dream smart. Let us help Marigold become what it was always meant to be."

Applause broke out in pockets — some eager, some uncertain.

Sophie felt her pulse thrum in her ears. She glanced at Cal. His jaw clenched, eyes storm-dark, but he hadn't spoken yet.

Then someone rose — old Mr. Nathaniel Reed. His voice wavered with age but not conviction.

"What happens to folks when those fancy shops move in?" he asked. "Where do we go when we can't afford our own homes anymore?"

The developer's man gave a pitying smile. "Sir, no one's talking about displacing anyone. We're offering opportunity."

Reed sat, unsatisfied.

Then Jeanine stood, arms crossed tight. "We've heard that before."

A low rumble of agreement.

Hester tried to regain order, but the room had tipped — split between hope and fear, gain and loss.

And still, Cal stayed silent — for now. But his moment was coming.

Cal's Speech

The room crackled with tension after the developer's pitch. A few hands clutched pamphlets with glossy promises; others sat clenched on knees, knuckles white, faces drawn tight with worry.

Hester cleared her throat, glancing toward Cal like she wasn't sure if she dared ask.

But Cal was already stepping forward, slow and deliberate.

He didn't have slides. He didn't need them.

The floorboards creaked beneath his boots as he faced the crowd — not polished or practiced, just steady. His hands hung loose at his sides, but Sophie, watching, could see the effort it took to unclench them.

He let the quiet stretch, let the weight of the moment settle over the room. When he spoke, his voice was low but carried, clear as a bell in the hush.

"I'm not a speaker," Cal began, glancing briefly at Sophie, then back at his neighbors. "You all know that. I'd rather build a porch or patch a roof than stand up here talkin' about futures and plans. But I can't stay quiet tonight."

He paused, gaze sweeping faces he'd known all his life.

"I've pounded nails into half the houses in this town. Helped raise the new church steeple after the storm. Sat up nights with neighbors when floodwaters came close. I've watched Marigold's paint peel and its windows board up. Watched folks I care about pack up and go, one by one, because they didn't see a future here anymore."

Cal's voice roughened, but he kept going.

"And yeah — those fancy renderings look nice. That hotel, those storefronts. I get the temptation. God knows I do. We're tired. We want something better. But better's gotta mean *ours*. Not someone else's idea of what we should be."

A murmur of agreement rippled at the edges of the room. Cal took a breath.

"My girl — Emma — she's ten. And every day I see her trying to picture a future here that isn't just dust and empty windows. That square out there? That's where she learned to ride her bike. Where she sells lemonade in the summer. Where she sketches buildings she's scared won't be here by the time she's grown."

His voice dropped softer, like he was sharing a secret meant just for the room.

"I don't want her to grow up thinking home's just a word folks use before they leave it behind. I want her to believe home's a place you fight for. That's what Sophie's plan is about. Not perfect, maybe not easy. But it's ours. Built with hands that know this town's shape, with hearts that don't want to see it sold off piece by piece."

Cal glanced at Sophie again, and this time, there was no distance in his gaze — just the quiet acknowledgment of shared purpose.

"I'm asking you not to take the quick money. Not to give up on Marigold just because we're tired. I'm asking you to remember what this place meant when you fell in love with it. When you built your lives here. When you stayed."

The room held its breath.

And then —

Old Mr. Reed tapped his cane against the floor, once, twice, slow and deliberate. Others followed — nods, murmurs, a soft chorus of assent that started at the edges and moved inward.

Cal let the silence answer, gave a small nod, and stepped back, hands still shaking just a little, but steadier than they'd been in a long time.

And beside him, Sophie felt something shift — not just in the room, but in herself.

She saw him, really saw him, and knew this: Marigold's strength wasn't in its buildings. It was in its people — and in moments like this, when one voice found the courage to speak for them all.

The meeting ended in a slow, reluctant unraveling — chairs scraping back, voices low, the weight of hard choices still hanging over the room. Outside, the night had turned crisp, the moon silvering the square's edges, softening the harsh lines of boarded windows and cracked stone.

Sophie stepped out onto the steps, drawing in a deep breath that tasted of woodsmoke and fallen leaves. The tension in her shoulders eased, just a little, as the cool air touched her skin.

Behind her, Cal emerged, his boots heavy on the worn planks. For a moment, neither of them spoke. "Hell of a night," he said finally, voice low.

Sophie managed a smile, small and tired. "You were incredible in there. You said what needed saying."

Cal shook his head. "I said what I could. Don't know if it's enough."

They stood in the quiet together, listening to the wind move through the empty square, the soft creak of the flagpole, the distant bark of a dog.

"Let me walk you," Cal said after a beat.

Sophie hesitated, then nodded. "I'd like that."

They set off down Main Street, their steps falling into an easy rhythm, the night folding around them like a shared coat.

For a while, they didn't speak — and the silence wasn't awkward. It felt earned.

At the corner near the hardware store, Cal stopped, resting a hand on the old iron railing, gaze sweeping the square.

"My dad used to bring me here on Saturdays," he said, voice soft with memory. "We'd get nails and sandpaper at the shop, and then he'd buy me a soda from the machine outside the post office. Said it tasted better because we earned it."

Sophie leaned against the railing beside him, touched by the image. "My mom and I would come here after church. We'd walk the square, just the two of us. She loved the fountain — said it made the town feel alive. Even when it started to crack, she'd sit on the edge like she didn't see the broken parts."

Cal glanced at her, seeing the quiet ache in her eyes.

"She sounds like she was a good woman."

"The best," Sophie said. "Coming back here… I thought I was doing it for her. Maybe I still am. But tonight, I realized I'm doing it for me too. Because I want Marigold to be what it could have been. What it still can be."

Cal was quiet for a moment, hands shoved deep in his pockets.

"I'm scared of what change means for Emma," he admitted. The words came slow, as if pulled from someplace deep. "I'm scared that in trying to save this place, I'll help bury what little of it still feels like home to her."

Sophie's heart softened, the distance between them shrinking not with steps, but with shared truth.

"She's lucky to have you," she said. "And whatever happens — I swear to you, I'll fight to make sure this is still her town."

Cal exhaled, the tension in his frame easing just a little.

They resumed walking, slower now. A cat darted across the road, its shadow long in the moonlight. Somewhere, a porch light flicked on, then off again.

When they reached the inn, they paused.

"I'm glad you're here," Cal said, surprising them both.

Sophie smiled — soft, but certain. "Me too."

Neither moved to leave. The night held them there, suspended in something fragile and unfinished.

Finally, Cal stepped back. "Get some rest. We've got a fight ahead."

Sophie nodded. "Good night, Cal."

"Night, Sophie.

Emma's Drawing

The next afternoon, the square was alive in a quiet, working way. The rival developer's flyers still fluttered in shop windows, but there was something else now — clusters of townsfolk talking in low voices, picking up litter, sweeping steps that hadn't seen a broom in months. A town at the edge of deciding.

Sophie had just finished measuring the storefront of what used to be the bakery when she heard a familiar voice behind her.

"Ms. Caldwell?"

She turned to see Emma standing there, hair pulled into a loose braid, a sketchbook hugged to her chest. She shifted from foot to foot, nervous but determined.

"Hi, Emma," Sophie said, softening immediately. "What can I do for you?"

Emma bit her lip, then stepped closer, glancing around as if making sure no one was watching.

"I—um—I made this," she said, holding out the sketchbook.

Sophie took it gently, flipping it open to the marked page.

The drawing took her breath for a second.

It was the square — but not as it was. As it *could* be. The fountain flowed again in pencil-soft streams, planters spilled over with blooms, shopfronts stood proud and whole. Kids played beneath the oaks, couples walked hand in hand. It was delicate and hopeful, lines etched with care.

"I didn't know you could draw like this," Sophie murmured.

Emma flushed. "It's just something I do sometimes. When I'm thinking."

"This is beautiful," Sophie said, meeting her gaze. "And it means the world that you shared it with me."

Emma ducked her head, then peeked up shyly. "Dad says you're trying to help. I wanted you to see what I hope for too. In case… in case it helps."

Sophie felt something in her chest ache, in that sweet, painful way hope can hurt.

"It helps more than you know," she said. "This—this is why I'm here. For this future."

Emma shuffled her feet. "Do you think we can really save it? The square?"

Sophie crouched to Emma's eye level, sketchbook balanced between them.

"I think it'll be hard. And I think we'll have to fight for it. But I believe in this place. And I believe in what *you* see."

Emma grinned, the first real smile Sophie had seen from her. "Dad's worried. He tries not to show it, but I can tell."

"I know," Sophie said gently. "I'll do my best to show him it's okay to hope."

Emma nodded, cheeks flushed with quiet pride.

"Will you keep this?" she asked, eyes wide.

"I'd be honored," Sophie said, hugging the sketchbook to her chest.

At that moment, Cal appeared at the edge of the square, wiping his hands on a rag, glancing over — and stopped short when he saw the two of them. His gaze softened at the sight of Emma's smile, at the way Sophie held the drawing like something precious.

Sophie straightened, and their eyes met across the space between.

Something shifted. Not all at once. But enough.

An Unplanned Dinner

It happened without planning — the way real moments do.

Sophie had stayed late in the square, walking it one more time as dusk bled into night. The sketch Emma had given her rested in her bag like a quiet promise. Sophie felt its weight with every step.

She was heading toward the inn when she spotted Cal near his truck, wiping down his tools by porch light. The night air smelled of cut grass and woodsmoke, the world soft and still in the fading light.

"You're still out?" he called, not unkindly.

"Could say the same for you," Sophie replied, crossing the small stretch of gravel that separated them.

Cal hesitated. "Emma's spending the night at Jeanine's. I had a few loose ends to finish. Then figured I'd make dinner. You eaten?"

Sophie blinked, surprised by the offer — or maybe by how much she wanted to say yes.

"No, actually. I lost track of time."

Cal shifted, wiping his hands on a rag. "It's nothing fancy. But there's enough."

Something unspoken passed between them. A shared weariness. A shared need for company, maybe.

"I'd like that," Sophie said.

His house was small but solid — worn wood floors, walls lined with books and old photos, the smell of cedar and coffee grounding it. A fire crackled low in the hearth, chasing off the night's chill.

Cal moved comfortably through the space, pulling plates from cabinets, setting out simple food: roasted chicken, cornbread, green beans from his garden. Sophie offered to help, but he shook his head.

"Sit. You've done enough today."

So she did. She watched as he worked, the easy competence of his hands, the way he moved like he was part of the house itself.

Over dinner, the conversation started haltingly — talk of town politics, of strategies, of the rival developer's latest moves. But somewhere between passing the cornbread and refilling glasses, it shifted.

Cal told her about Emma's first art show at school — how nervous she'd been, how proud he was.

Sophie shared a story about her mother teaching her to bake bread, the kitchen filled with flour and laughter.

They laughed together — real laughter, the kind that surprises you when you didn't know you needed it.

When the plates were cleared, they found themselves standing at the sink, shoulder to shoulder, washing and drying dishes in quiet rhythm.

Their hands brushed once — a fleeting touch that neither of them meant, but neither quite forgot. Sophie felt her breath catch; Cal stilled for the briefest moment before passing her a plate.

The air between them changed. Softer. Charged.

As Cal set the last dish on the rack, he glanced at her, something unguarded in his eyes.

"Thank you," Sophie said, her voice low.

"For what?"

"For this. For letting me in tonight. For trusting me, even a little."

Cal looked down at his hands, then back at her.

"I'm trying," he said simply.

Sophie smiled — small, but true.

Outside, the wind picked up, rattling the windows gently. Inside, the house felt warm, the kind of warmth that comes not from the fire, but from the company.

Neither moved for a moment, caught in the stillness — in what almost was, in what might be, if either of them dared.

Finally, Cal stepped back, breaking the spell.

"I should walk you out," he said.

"I can find my way," Sophie replied, but she didn't argue when he grabbed his jacket and opened the door.

Outside, the stars were sharp and bright, the square visible in the distance — a shape waiting to be saved.

Cal lingered at the edge… "Night, Sophie," he said, his voice quieter than before.

"Night, Cal."

And as she walked away, she realized her heart had opened wider — and with it, the risk of breaking had grown too.

A Phone Call That Changes Everything

The night air still clung to Sophie's skin as she let herself into her room at the Marigold House. She moved on autopilot — keys on the table, jacket draped over the chair, bag set down with care as if the drawing inside might break.

Her chest felt full in a way it hadn't in a long time. The quiet warmth of Cal's kitchen lingered — the low hum of conversation, that small touch at the sink, the easy way they'd laughed together like they'd done it a hundred times before.

Sophie stood at the window, looking out at the square. In the moonlight, it almost looked whole again.

The broken fountain cast long shadows, but the shape of it remained. Like hope.

Her phone buzzed on the nightstand.

Sophie blinked, surprised by the sound. The hour was late. A pulse of unease shot through her as she crossed to pick it up.

The name on the screen made her stomach twist: *Anderson — Prime Heritage Capital.*

The investor who'd backed her vision. The man who'd promised support when no one else had.

She answered, voice tight. "Hi, Frank. Everything okay?"

There was a pause on the other end — too long, too telling.

"Sophie. I wish I had better news."

The room seemed to shrink around her.

"What's going on?"

Frank's voice was all polished regret. "The board's getting cold feet. The rival developer's leaning hard — lobbying, offering them co-investment options, promising faster returns. The optics of fighting them in court over that injunction spooked a few people. They're seeing risk where they used to see vision."

Sophie gripped the edge of the desk, knuckles white. "Frank. We have a plan. We have the community starting to rally. You can't just—"

"I'm trying, Sophie. I am. But I've got partners to answer to. There's talk of pulling the funding entirely if this doesn't shift in the next week. I thought you should know."

Her mind raced — through the weeks of work, the promises made, the people she'd convinced, the trust she'd barely begun to earn. And now, with one phone call, the foundation cracked beneath her feet.

"You said you believed in this," she said, her voice quieter now, but steady.

"I do. But belief doesn't always pay the bills. I'll stall as long as I can — but get something on the board fast. Something public. Something that shows you can win this."

And then he was gone. The line clicked dead.

Sophie stood there, phone limp in her hand, the quiet of the room pressing against her like a weight.

Outside, the square waited, silent and scarred.

She turned, sank onto the edge of the bed, and let herself feel it — the fear, the frustration, the raw unfairness of it all.

But only for a moment.

Because she wasn't that girl who ran from Marigold once upon a time. She was the woman who'd come back. Who'd made promises.

She wiped at her eyes, squared her shoulders, and pulled out Emma's drawing, laying it on the desk in front of her.

"We're not done," Sophie whispered. "Not even close."

The square would have to be saved piece by piece, heart by heart — and Sophie Caldwell would find a way.

Chapter 8

Crossroads

The square felt different at dawn. The hope that had started to blossom in its cracked sidewalks and battered benches seemed smothered now, as if the air itself carried the weight of disappointment.

Sophie hadn't slept. She'd spent the night at the small desk in her room at the Marigold House, laptop open, papers spread like fallen leaves. The screen glowed with spreadsheets, revised budgets, desperate notes to contacts who might — *might* — have connections to someone willing to help.

Her coffee had gone cold hours ago.

She dialed and redialed numbers: old colleagues, grant officers, the sympathetic lawyer who'd helped file the injunction. Most answered with regret; some didn't answer at all.

Outside her window, the town woke up. Shop doors opened, porch lights flicked off, and the rival developer's flyers caught the morning breeze, flapping like warnings.

By noon, the gossip had spread.

Sophie felt it when she stepped into the square: the way heads turned, the way conversation dipped as she passed. A woman at the café window whispered something behind her hand. A man on the hardware store steps shook his head, muttering, "Always the same story. Big promises. Big letdowns."

Sophie forced herself to keep walking, even though each word felt like a pebble in her shoe, small but relentless.

The rival developer wasn't wasting time. Their rep moved smoothly through town, meeting shop owners, offering incentives. Quick repairs to storefronts. Rent forgiveness for struggling businesses. Cash offers that felt like lifelines — with strings no one wanted to see until it was too late.

At the barbershop, Mr. Reed stood outside, arms folded, watching it all. When Sophie passed, he called out softly, not unkind.

"Town's got a choice to make, Miss Caldwell. Wouldn't trade places with you."

Sophie paused, met his gaze.

"No one said saving something was easy," she said quietly.

He nodded once. "True enough."

But as she walked on, the doubts crept closer. The rival's money spoke louder than her promises. And with each handshake, each nod from a weary business owner, Sophie felt the ground shift.

At the end of the day, she stood at the fountain, the square emptying around her. The sun slipped low, casting everything in gold and shadow.

Her phone buzzed in her pocket — another investor saying no, politely but firmly.

Sophie closed her eyes, drew a breath that tasted of dust and woodsmoke.

And then she opened her notebook, flipped to a clean page, and began to write. Ideas. Names. Anything that might keep this fight alive.

Because giving up wasn't an option. Not now. Not ever.

Cal's Doubts Resurface

Cal watched from his workshop window as the sun dipped low, the square painted in amber light that did nothing to soften its worn edges.

He'd heard the talk all day — the muttered doubts, the sharper words that followed Sophie's name. He'd seen the rival developer's man shaking hands, slipping papers across counters, making promises with a smile that didn't reach his eyes.

And he'd seen Sophie — moving through the square like she was carrying the weight of the world, shoulders tight, steps slower than before.

Cal scrubbed a hand down his face. What were they doing?

He'd let himself believe. In Sophie. In a future that didn't feel like watching the town he loved fall apart board by board.

But was he fooling himself?

A knock at the open door startled him. Sophie stood there, the last of the sunlight catching in her hair, fatigue written in every line of her face.

"We need to talk," she said.

"Yeah," Cal said, stepping aside. "I reckon we do."

They sat across from each other at the workbench, the air between them thick with everything unsaid.

"I'm doing everything I can," Sophie began, voice low but firm. "I'm making calls. Reworking numbers. I haven't stopped trying."

Cal let out a breath, slow and rough. "I know you're trying. I see it. But what if it's not enough?"

Sophie blinked, caught off guard. "You think I don't ask myself that every minute? But what's the alternative — let the rival developer gut this place?"

Cal stood, pacing, hands on his hips.

"You don't get it. You can leave. You can go back to your city, your work. Me — I stay. I see what's left after the dust settles."

"That's not fair," Sophie said, rising to meet him, her own temper fraying. "You think I don't care because I wasn't born on this square? Because I left once? I came back. I stayed. I'm fighting for this just like you are."

Cal turned, frustration and something rawer in his gaze.

"I don't want Emma growing up watching this town die slow. But I'm scared, Sophie. Scared I let myself hope for something that was never real."

That stopped her cold.

"You're not the only one who's scared," she said softly. "I'm terrified. But I'm here. I'm not walking away."

They stood close now, the tension between them no longer just anger — it was everything unspoken, everything they didn't dare admit.

Cal's hand twitched at his side, as if he might reach for her. But he didn't.

Instead, he shook his head, stepped back, and the space between them felt cavernous.

"I need air," he muttered, striding toward the door.

Sophie let him go. She stood at the front of the workshop, heart pounding, fighting the sting of tears she refused to shed.

Because this wasn't just about plans or buildings anymore.

It was about trust. About risking something deeper than either of them had planned.

Emma's Intervention

Later that evening, with the air thickening with pine and woodsmoke, Cal stood on the porch, arms braced on the railing, staring out at nothing. The stars were just beginning to show, pale and tentative.

Inside, the house was quiet, save for the soft shuffle of Emma's feet as she padded toward the door. She paused in the glow of the porch light, clutching her sketchpad to her chest.

"Daddy?"

Cal turned, his expression softening the moment he saw her.

"Hey, bug. What're you doing up?"

Emma hesitated, then stepped out onto the porch, bare feet whispering against the old boards. She held out the sketchpad.

"I made another one," she said, voice small but steady.

Cal took it gently, like it was something fragile. He flipped to the page she'd marked.

The drawing was simple, but it hit him square in the chest.

The square — the fountain restored, flowers blooming, shop windows lit. And in the center, three figures: a tall man, a woman with hair like Sophie's, and a girl holding both their hands.

"I didn't know what else to do," Emma said, words tumbling out now. "I heard people talking today — at the store, outside the library. They were saying mean things about Sophie. That she's lying, that she'll leave like everyone else. And I just… I wanted you to see. What I see. What I hope."

Cal swallowed hard, the lump in his throat making it hard to speak.

"Bug, you don't have to worry about this stuff. It's not your job."

Emma shook her head, fierce and earnest.

"But it *is*, Daddy. It's our town. And I like her. She makes me feel like things could be good again. Like you don't have to do it all alone."

Her voice broke a little on the last word.

Cal sank to one knee, pulling her close, her small arms wrapping around his neck.

"You're not supposed to be the one holding *me* up," he said, voice rough with emotion.

Emma leaned back just enough to look him in the eye.

"Then don't push away the people who want to help."

Cal let out a breath that felt like it carried years. He looked down at the sketch again — the hope drawn in every line, the future his daughter dreamed of.

"Okay," he said quietly. "Okay, bug. I hear you."

Emma smiled, the weight lifting from her shoulders.

"Will you tell her? That you believe in her?"

Cal stood, ruffling her hair.

"I'll try, bug. That's a promise."

And as they went inside together, the sketch still in his hand, Cal felt something shift — not all the way, not yet. But enough.

The town hall overflowed with bodies and tension. Folding chairs scraped the old wood floors as people squeezed in — shopkeepers, farmers, teachers, retirees, teenagers clutching petitions Emma had passed around. The air smelled of sawdust, coffee, and nerves.

Sophie stood at the front, heart pounding so hard she thought it might shake her voice loose. The long oak table before her felt like a barrier and an anchor.

She'd come without slides. Without plans rolled in tubes or glossy renderings to distract from what really mattered.

Tonight, it was just her and her promise.

She let her gaze sweep the room — saw the hope in Emma's face, the worry in Mr. Reed's, the skepticism in Councilwoman Boyd's. And Cal, standing near the back, arms crossed, expression guarded but present.

Sophie took a breath, feeling the room's weight settle on her shoulders.

"I came to Marigold thinking I could fix things with plans and funding," she began, her voice steady despite the tightness in her chest. "But what I've learned is that saving this town isn't about what I can bring in. It's about what we build together — or what we lose if we don't try."

Murmurs rippled through the crowd, not hostile, but wary.

"I'm not asking you to trust me because of my mother, or because I grew up here for a while, or because I've fought for funding. I'm asking you to trust that I'll stay. That I'll work. That I'll listen. That I'll be here *with* you."

She let the silence stretch, the words sink in.

Then Cal stepped forward.

At first, he didn't speak. Just stood beside Sophie, hands in his pockets, eyes sweeping the crowd like he was looking for the right place to start.

"When I was a kid," he said finally, "this square was where everything happened. Parades, markets, first dates, last goodbyes. It's where my dad taught me to patch a tire, where I taught Emma to ride a bike. I've spent my life trying to hold this town together one nail at a time.

"I don't like outsiders telling us what we need. But I've watched Sophie work. I've seen her stay when she could've run. And I believe she means it when she says this isn't just a project. It's a promise."

The room hushed, listening.

"That's why I'm offering up my business — the shop, the land — as temporary collateral. It won't cover everything, not for long. But maybe it buys us time. And I believe she'll use that time the right way. I believe in her. And I believe in us."

A shocked silence followed — then the murmurs began again, different now.

Councilwoman Boyd cleared her throat.

"Well," she said, voice softer than before, "seems we have ourselves a decision."

The council huddled, voices low but urgent. The room held its breath.

Minutes passed like hours.

Finally, Hester Boyd faced the crowd.

"The council votes in favor of moving forward with Ms. Caldwell's plan — contingent on securing new funding within thirty days. We know this doesn't fix it all. But we're giving this one more chance."

Relief crashed through Sophie like a wave. The room erupted — applause, tears, the buzz of hope reigniting.

Cal turned to her, and for a moment they just looked at each other — partners now, in the truest sense.

An Unexpected Ally

The applause had faded, but the energy in the town hall lingered — a mix of hope, disbelief, and the first fragile threads of unity.

Sophie stood rooted to the spot, the council's decision still echoing in her ears. She felt Cal's presence beside her, solid and grounding, but the weight of what came next loomed large.

Thirty days. New funding. Or it all falls apart.

People were milling about now, voices low but urgent, hands clapping shoulders, heads shaking in wonder. The square's future had pivoted in a single vote, and everyone knew it.

Jeanine moved through the crowd like a current beneath the surface — quiet, purposeful, unseen until she was there at Sophie's side.

"You did good tonight," Jeanine said, her voice low, so it didn't carry beyond them.

Sophie gave a breathless laugh, the tension making it sound more like a gasp. "I don't know if good will be good enough."

Jeanine nodded once, as if she'd expected that answer. "That's why I'm here."

She set down her ever-present canvas tote, rummaging inside until she pulled out an old ledger — the kind with a cracked leather cover and yellowing pages.

"The historical society isn't just old photographs and bake sales," Jeanine said, flipping to a marked page. "We've got a trust fund. Started generations ago, meant to be a last-resort preservation fund for the square. Problem is, folks forgot it existed. The records got buried under years of turnover and neglect."

Sophie blinked, hope flaring so fast it hurt.

"Why hasn't anyone mentioned this before?"

Jeanine gave her a wry look. "Because until tonight, I wasn't sure we had someone worth mentioning it to."

Sophie's throat tightened. "Jeanine—"

"Don't thank me yet," Jeanine said, snapping the ledger shut and holding it out. "The paperwork's a mess. The fund's modest — not enough to finish what you're dreaming of, but enough to buy you breathing room. A bridge. You'll still need more, but this could stop the rival from buying up more pieces of the square while you work."

Sophie took the ledger carefully, as if it might shatter in her hands.

"This… this could change everything."

Jeanine's smile was small but real. "I thought it might."

From the corner of her eye, Sophie saw Cal watching them — wary at first, then curious, then something like cautious hope dawning in his gaze.

"I'll help you untangle it," Jeanine added. "I've got contacts in the state preservation office. They'll know the legal steps to access the fund properly. And I'll speak up. At the next meeting. In the paper. Wherever it counts."

Sophie could only nod, overwhelmed by the unexpected generosity, the quiet strength of this woman who had been watching, waiting, and now — finally — stepping in.

"I don't know how to thank you," Sophie said at last.

Jeanine shrugged. "Don't. Just keep showing up. That's all we ask in Marigold."

A Quiet Moment

The town hall had emptied slowly — chairs scraped back, voices faded, doors creaked shut behind lingering groups reluctant to leave the charged air of decision.

Outside, the night had settled over Marigold like a soft quilt. Crickets thrummed in the distance. The breeze carried the scent of magnolia and cut grass, mingled with the faint tang of motor oil from an old truck idling somewhere down the street.

Sophie stepped onto the worn stone steps, the ledger Jeanine had given her pressed to her chest. The square spread before her, bathed in silvered moonlight, the fountain's broken rim casting long shadows.

She drew a breath that trembled at the edges.

"Hell of a night."

Cal's voice, low and rough, came from behind her. He joined her on the steps, hands shoved deep in his pockets, head tilted to the stars.

Sophie nodded, not trusting herself to speak.

For a moment they stood side by side in the hush, two silhouettes framed against the square that had brought them together and threatened to break them apart.

Cal shifted, glanced at her.

"You did good in there," he said quietly. "Not just the speech. The fight. The staying." Sophie nodded. But she knew — Cal's gesture, the council's vote — it was all a bridge, not a landing. The real work hadn't even begun.

Sophie gave a soft laugh, dry and a little bitter. "For now. Tomorrow I start the scramble for more funding. Again."

Cal's mouth curved — not quite a smile, but close. "You'll find a way. You're stubborn like that."

She turned to face him fully, the moon catching the glint of exhaustion in her eyes. "You're not so bad at staying yourself."

Their gazes locked — and for a heartbeat, the night held its breath.

Cal's hand lifted slightly, as if he might reach for her cheek, tuck that loose strand of hair behind her ear the way he'd wanted to a hundred times. But he stopped short, fingers curling into a fist instead.

The ghost of another night, another almost — Lena, quiet and graceful, her absence still echoing — flickered through him. He wasn't ready. Not yet. Not with this weight between them.

Sophie saw the movement, felt the pull between them like a thread stretched taut.

"Cal—" she began, unsure what she meant to say.

But he shook his head, soft and rueful.

"Not tonight," he said, voice low. "Too much in the air already." His gaze held hers, steady but shadowed. She knew about Lena, at least the outline of it. But not the weight Cal carried, not the ache behind his silences. And somehow, it was there between them anyway — unspoken, but heavy as truth.

She nodded, understanding more than she could say.

And so they stood in the quiet, side by side, watching the town they both loved and feared losing — together, but not quite touching.

The promise of something more shimmered between them, unspoken, waiting for the right moment.

When Sophie finally turned to leave, Cal fell into step beside her, walking her into the quiet — not speaking, not touching, but there. And for now, that was enough.

Chapter 9

Rising Together

The night had not been kind to Sophie. Long after the town hall doors had closed, after the last voices had faded into the dark, she had lain in her narrow bed at the Marigold House, staring at the cracked ceiling, listening to the sigh of the night wind through the trees.

Sleep came in fits, chased away by the weight in her chest. Not just the worry — though there was plenty of that — but the ache of questions she hadn't dared name until now.

Cal.

She could still feel the nearness of him on the town hall steps, the unspoken pull between them, the warmth that might have been his hand brushing her cheek — if he hadn't stopped short. *Not tonight,* he'd said. And she had understood, or thought she had.

But now, in the quiet dark, her mind turned it over and over. Why *not* tonight? Was it just the tension of the meeting, the exhaustion of the fight — or something more?

Someone more?

She knew so little of his heart. He had given pieces of himself in moments: in the workshop, at the square, in the way he stood beside her when no one else would. But there were spaces she couldn't see, shadows where his past lived. Shadows where Lena's name might be written, if only she knew to look.

Sophie swallowed hard, eyes stinging with unshed tears. *I'm falling for a man whose heart might not be his to give.*

And still, she felt drawn — helplessly, undeniably — as if some part of her had been waiting for him long before she came to Marigold.

When at last the first pale light of morning crept through the lace curtains, Sophie turned her face to it, weary but resolved. There was work to do, and she would do it — no matter where Cal's heart truly lay.

A New Day, A New Resolve

The morning light spilled through the lace curtains of Sophie's room at the Marigold House, casting soft patterns on the worn wooden floor. For a moment, she lay still, listening to the quiet hum of the town waking — birdsong, the creak of a porch swing somewhere, the distant thud of a screen door.

Her first conscious thought was of the vote. The ledger. The look on Cal's face when the council said yes. And the weight of the "now what?" that had settled over her as she'd driven back to the inn.

With a sigh, she swung her legs out of bed, bracing for the day's uncertainties.

But as she crossed to the door, she noticed something that hadn't been there the night before: a small stack of folded papers, slipped beneath the frame.

Frowning, she knelt and gathered them — handwritten notes, their edges creased, the ink in places smudged as if by hurried hands.

She opened the first.

"My granddad laid the bricks on Main Street. If you need help patching them, I'm your man. — Joe Walters"

The next:

"We can't offer much, but our Sunday bake sale proceeds are yours if it helps. — The First Methodist Ladies"

And another:

"I wasn't sure about you at first. I'm still not. But my boy says you listened to him about the skate park. That counts. Count me in. — Troy Henson"

Note after note — offers of tools, time, small donations, words of cautious but genuine encouragement.

Sophie sank onto the edge of the bed, heart swelling, throat tight. She hadn't expected this. Not yet. Maybe not ever.

They're with us, she thought. *Or at least willing to try.*

A knock startled her from the moment.

"Miss Caldwell?" Mrs. Clemens called through the door. "You might want to look out your window."

Sophie crossed to the glass, pulling back the curtain.

The square below was no longer still.

Here and there, people moved with quiet purpose. A pair of teenagers swept the sidewalks with old brooms. A farmer in coveralls pruned the overgrown rose bushes near the library steps. Mr. Reed stood on a ladder, wiping down the cracked sign above the barbershop.

A pickup backed in near the fountain, its bed full of tools and buckets.

The town was stirring.

Marigold was stirring.

Sophie pressed her palm to the windowpane, a tear escaping despite herself.

Cal Steps Up

The square buzzed with an energy Sophie hadn't felt in Marigold since she was a child. The hum of voices, the clatter of tools, the scrape of rakes and brooms filled the air.

She found Cal near the fountain, sleeves rolled, a toolbelt slung low on his hips, clipboard in hand. His hair stuck to his forehead, and his shirt was damp with sweat despite the morning chill. But there was a light in his eyes she hadn't seen before — not defiance, not suspicion, but purpose.

"You organized all this?" Sophie asked, taking in the clusters of people working in loose teams.

Cal shrugged, glancing at the clipboard. "Folks needed a starting point. I gave them one. Square Clean-Up Day. Nothing fancy. Just work."

He handed her a pair of gloves — sturdy leather ones, worn but solid.

"You ready?"

Sophie nodded, slipping them on.

They fell into rhythm without thinking. Cal showed her how to sand the splintered benches near the fountain, his movements efficient, precise. She matched his pace, arms aching but heart lightening with each pass of the sandpaper.

Nearby, kids carried trash bags twice their size, giggling as they competed to see who could fill theirs fastest.

At one point, Cal climbed a ladder to hammer loose trim back onto the library's porch. Sophie steadied it, craning her neck to watch him work, the sun turning his hair copper at the edges.

"You're good at this," she called up.

"At fixing what's broken?" His voice floated down with a dry chuckle. "Plenty of practice."

Later, as they knelt side by side replanting one of the square's long-neglected planters, Sophie stole a glance at him — dirt on his cheek, hands moving with care as he eased fragile roots into place.

"You always this bossy on your clean-up days?" she teased.

He smirked, wiping sweat from his brow. "Only when people don't follow orders."

Their laughter blended with the square's new heartbeat: the scrape of metal against stone, the swish of brooms, the creak of old hinges coaxed back to life.

Around noon, Cal called a break.

He produced a cooler from his truck and passed around bottles of water and sandwiches wrapped in wax paper — simple food, but shared with an ease that felt like family.

Sophie found herself seated on the edge of the fountain, sipping water, watching the townspeople gather.

Teenagers flopped onto the grass. Old-timers leaned on canes, catching their breath. Parents wiped sweat from their brows and smiled at their kids, who chased each other through the cleaned-up square like it was already theirs again.

Cal settled beside her, gaze on the scene before them.

"Not bad for a day's work," he said quietly.

"Not bad at all," Sophie agreed, and meant it with all her heart.

Emma Finds Her Voice

The midday sun slanted across the square, casting shadows beneath the benches and newly pruned trees. Lunch break had mellowed the workers into small clusters — some sprawled on the grass, others leaning against shopfronts, their tools set aside for the moment.

A folding table near the fountain held an assortment of sandwiches, apples, and paper cups of lemonade, set out by the garden club and the church ladies. The air smelled of cut grass and fresh paint — and something else: the first faint whiff of hope.

Sophie sipped her lemonade, seated cross-legged beneath the old oak that anchored the square's corner. Cal was off to one side, conferring with Mr. Reed about how best to brace the sagging bandstand.

A lull settled over the square as conversations quieted and shade grew long. Sophie leaned back against the tree, unaware that something was about to shift.

She didn't notice Emma at first. The girl had been quiet all morning, flitting between the clean-up teams, sketchbook always tucked under one arm, scribbling now and then, watching everything.

It was the hush that drew Sophie's attention.

Emma had climbed the steps of the bandstand, her slim frame

dwarfed by the structure's age-worn timbers. She stood awkwardly for a second, then cleared her throat.

The low murmur of conversation ebbed. Heads turned.

"Um — hi," Emma began, voice soft but steady. "I just wanted to say something."

Cal froze where he stood, surprise flickering across his face. Sophie's heart tightened, watching him — watching her.

Emma took a breath, the kind you take before diving into deep water.

"My name's Emma Bennett. Some of you know me from school, or church, or because my dad's fixed your roof or your porch." A small smile tugged at the corners of her mouth. "I've lived here my whole life. And I don't want to live anywhere else."

The square held its breath.

"I know I'm just a kid," Emma went on, voice gaining strength, "but I see what's happening. I see buildings falling down, stores closing, people moving away because they think there's nothing left. But there is. I see it. We're fixing it right now. Together."

Sophie blinked back tears, glancing at Cal. His jaw was tight, his eyes shining.

"My dad always says you don't quit on something you love, just because it's hard," Emma said. "And I think we all love Marigold. So let's not quit. Let's not give up."

For a moment, silence. Then someone clapped — slow, steady — and others joined in.

Emma flushed pink, but her smile grew.

She held up her sketchbook, flipping it around so everyone could see.

It was a drawing of the square — not as it was now, but as it could be: the fountain sparkling, flowers spilling from planters, children playing, shop windows bright and welcoming. And at the heart of it, drawn in fine, careful lines, were three small figures — Emma, Cal, and

Sophie — standing together beneath the old oak tree.

Sophie felt her breath hitch, a lump rising in her throat.

Cal stepped forward, climbing the bandstand steps, placing a steadying hand on his daughter's shoulder.

"You've got more sense than most grown-ups I know," he said quietly, pride softening his voice.

The applause swelled — not wild or raucous, but real.

And as Emma stepped down into the crowd, Sophie knew this moment mattered. The square wasn't just theirs now. It belonged to *everyone* who chose to stay and fight for it.

The Media Takes Notice

By late afternoon, the square glowed in the golden light of early evening. Dust motes danced in the air, stirred by the steady rhythm of brooms and the scrape of shovels. The scent of fresh-cut grass mingled with sawdust, paint, and the tang of lemonade spilled beneath the bandstand.

Sophie leaned against a lamppost, wiping sweat from her brow with the hem of her shirt, surveying the square with equal parts exhaustion and wonder. What had felt impossible only a few days ago now felt — just barely — within reach.

A camera shutter clicked.

She turned, startled.

A woman stood near the fountain, camera raised, capturing the scene with practiced ease: Cal atop scaffolding tightening bolts on the repaired bandstand, a group of teens painting the fence around the little park, Mrs. Clemens handing out paper cups of sweet tea to the tired but smiling workers.

"Hope you don't mind," the woman said, lowering the camera. She had sharp eyes, quick hands, a messenger bag slung across one shoulder. "Ellie Thomas. *Marigold Gazette*. Figured it was time this effort got a little love in print."

Sophie blinked, caught off guard. "Of course not. I just didn't think…"

Ellie grinned. "Didn't think anyone was paying attention? You'd be surprised what people notice when a town starts to wake up."

She moved through the square, snapping photos — a kid balancing on the edge of the fountain's basin, Cal's dog stretched out in the shade, the worn sign of the hardware store with its freshly washed windows.

"What's the story you're writing?" Sophie asked, falling into step beside her.

Ellie lifted the camera again. "A simple one. People showing up. Doing the work. Reminding themselves and everyone else what this place can be."

By the next morning, the article ran in the *Gazette*:

MARIGOLD RISES: SQUARE CLEAN-UP SPARKS NEW HOPE

The words were plain, but the photos spoke louder — the square alive with color and effort, faces familiar and proud, the banner Emma had drawn in the background of one shot like a promise made visible.

What Sophie didn't expect came next.

The piece was shared — first in neighboring towns, then picked up by a regional blog that covered small-town revitalizations. Comments rolled in:

"Good to see a town fight for itself."

"Reminds me of when our main street came back to life."

"Rooting for Marigold!"

And then — an email, flagged as important in Sophie's inbox.

Subject: *Re: Marigold Project*

From: Dana L., Regional Revitalization Fund

Sophie — I read about your team's work. Let's revisit your proposal. Call me.

— Dana L.

Sophie stared at the screen, pulse quickening.

She looked out the window at the square below, where Cal was showing a pair of volunteers how to anchor a new bench. His sleeves were rolled, his hair mussed, but his posture spoke of quiet pride.

For the first time, it wasn't just *their* eyes on Marigold.

It was the world's.

The council's vote had bought them thirty days, and Cal's offer of his business had helped tip the scale. But none of that money had come through yet. This? This was just time — time they were using to prove Marigold was worth saving.

A Turning Point for Sophie and Cal

The square lay quiet under the first blush of dusk, the day's clatter and hum faded to a peaceful hush. The volunteers had gone home, leaving behind the scent of sawdust, paint, and sun-warmed earth.

Sophie stood at the base of the scaffolding, head tipped back, watching Cal secure the last of the bandstand's crossbeams. His silhouette was outlined against a lavender sky, the setting sun streaking gold across his shoulders.

"You planning to stay up there all night?" she called, a smile in her voice.

Cal looked down, grinning as he wiped his hands on his jeans. "Thinking about it. The view's not bad."

"Move over, then."

Before he could object, Sophie was climbing — slow at first, then steadier as the boards held firm beneath her boots. When she reached the top, she settled beside him on the narrow planks, legs dangling over the edge.

The square stretched before them, bathed in soft light. The fountain, cleaned and cleared of debris, glinted like a promise. The planters, filled with fresh soil, waited for blooms. The benches gleamed where the old varnish had been sanded away and replaced.

"It looks… almost new," Sophie said quietly.

Cal shook his head. "It looks like home."

They sat in silence for a long moment, breathing in the cool evening air. A breeze stirred, carrying the scent of honeysuckle from somewhere near the café.

Cal rested his arms on his knees, gaze distant.

"I never told you about Lena," he said, voice low.

Sophie glanced at him, surprised by the sudden intimacy.

"My wife. Emma's mom." He exhaled slowly, like letting out a weight. "She loved this town even more than I do. Saw good in every crack, every broken thing. After she got sick, we'd sit here — this very spot — and she'd talk about how we'd fix it all. Together. When she got better."

His voice caught.

"She didn't get better."

Sophie's heart ached. "I'm so sorry, Cal."

He nodded, jaw tight. "I guess I kept trying to hold on to what she loved. But it slipped away anyway. The town. The square. I thought if I could just… patch it, somehow I'd be keeping her with us. But it wasn't enough. And I hated feeling like I was losing twice."

Sophie didn't speak. She just listened, letting him have the space he'd never taken before.

When he looked at her, his eyes were clearer than she'd ever seen them.

"And then you showed up," he said. "And I didn't want to hope. I was mad at you for making me want to."

Sophie's throat tightened.

"I was mad at myself for wanting to," she admitted. She turned back to the square. "I left this place because I thought I had to. Thought I could outrun what it took from my family. But I couldn't. It's in me. And now I'm scared that wanting something good — here, with you, with this town — means I'll lose again."

The breeze stirred again, lifting a loose strand of her hair.

Cal reached out, almost without thinking, tucking it behind her ear.

His fingers brushed her cheek — a touch so light, so fleeting, but it sent a shiver down Sophie's spine.

They held each other's gaze, the square spread below them like a shared secret.

Cal's voice was a whisper. "I don't want to lose again either."

And in that quiet, they both understood — this was the moment they'd stopped being two people fighting for the same ground and started being two people fighting for each other.

The First Signs of Transformation

Morning came soft and bright, the kind of day that felt like a fresh start even before the coffee brewed. The square smelled of damp earth and sawdust, of cut grass and something sweeter: possibility.

Sophie arrived early, walking the length of Main Street in the hush before Marigold fully woke. She ran her fingers along the smooth wood of a freshly mended bench, paused to admire the way the repaired planters caught the morning light.

Cal was already at the fountain. He stood with Emma, both of them streaked with dust and sweat from their efforts. A small crew of volunteers milled nearby, hauling buckets and tools, laughter punctuating their work.

Sophie crossed to join them, heart lifting at the sight.

"What's the plan?" she asked, nodding toward the fountain.

Cal's grin was boyish, free. "You'll see."

Emma bounced on her toes, unable to contain her excitement.

Together, they watched as the team fitted a temporary water line — a humble rig cobbled from hoses, borrowed parts, and ingenuity. A volunteer gave the signal, and the water rushed in.

For a breathless beat, nothing.

Then — a trickle, a sputter, and at last a clear stream arched from the fountain's center, catching the sunlight in a burst of silver and gold. Cheers rose from the square as the water flowed, a fragile, hopeful song after so many silent years.

Sophie felt tears prick her eyes. The sound, the shimmer — it was everything she'd pictured, and more.

Emma clapped her hands, laughing, the pure, bright kind of laugh that carried across the square and made grown men smile. Cal looked at his daughter, then at Sophie, and for once let his guard down completely.

"I never thought I'd see that again," he said quietly.

"It's just a start," Sophie said, voice thick with emotion.

"That's more than we had yesterday."

The square seemed to change before their eyes. Children appeared as if summoned by the sound of the water, chasing one another around the fountain's base. An old man set up a folding chair in the shade, harmonica in hand, notes drifting on the breeze.

From the café — closed for years but now with its door propped open for cleaning — came the warm scent of brewing coffee. Someone strung up a battered radio, and soft music mingled with the splash of water and the low hum of conversation.

Mrs. Clemens appeared with a tray of lemonade, handing out cups with the quiet pride of someone who'd almost stopped believing but hadn't.

A banner, hastily painted the night before by Jeanine and her garden club, now stretched across Main Street between two lampposts:

MARIGOLD RISING

Sophie stood at the fountain's edge, the spray cool against her cheeks, and let herself believe — really believe — for the first time that this could work.

Cal touched her elbow gently, drawing her gaze.

"We did this," he said.

"No," Sophie said, shaking her head. "*They* did this. We just reminded them how."

They stood together, watching as the square filled not just with people, but with life.

And for that moment, at least, Marigold was whole again.

Chapter 10

The Grand Reopening

Sophie woke before dawn, the soft gray of morning filtering through the thin curtains of her room at the Marigold House. For a moment, she lay still, listening to the quiet hum of the town holding its breath. Today wasn't just another step in the project. It was the day Marigold would see what it had done — what they had done together.

Her heart pounded with a tangle of emotions she could barely name: anticipation, pride, and that old, familiar flicker of doubt. Would it be enough? Would the square's new life be met with joy — or with the sharp scrutiny that had shadowed every step of the journey?

Outside, the first rays of sun painted the square in hues of rose gold. Sophie rose and crossed to the window, fingers brushing the glass as she gazed out at the scene unfolding below.

The square was already stirring. Vendors arrived in pickups and vans, unloading tables, crates of fresh flowers, hand-lettered signs. A food truck hummed to life near the café, the aroma of frying batter mingling with morning air that smelled of grass and sawdust. Musicians tuned guitars and adjusted mic stands on the bandstand, their notes tentative at first, then bolder as the sound system came alive.

From every corner, townspeople emerged — some in their Sunday best, others in jeans and work boots, sleeves rolled as they strung bunting from lampposts and draped string lights across the bandstand railings.

The square, once hollow and silent, pulsed now with the heartbeat of a town coming back to itself.

Sophie dressed quickly — simple jeans, a crisp white blouse she'd saved for the occasion, boots that could handle the cobblestones — and stepped out into the morning with a breath drawn deep into her lungs.

On the inn's porch, Mrs. Clemens rocked slowly in her chair, knitting needles clicking softly. She gave Sophie a small nod — not warm, not cold, but with the quiet dignity of someone who'd seen many mornings like this and knew their weight.

Sophie crossed the square, offering a hand here, a word of thanks there, but mostly letting herself soak it in: the laughter of children helping hang banners, the bark of a dog chasing pigeons from the fountain's edge, the clink of mugs as the café reopened its doors to early customers.

Then, a small voice called her name.

Emma stood at the edge of the bandstand, a bundle of wildflowers cradled in her arms — daisies, black-eyed Susans, and sprigs of Queen Anne's lace gathered fresh from some hidden corner of Marigold.

"These are for you," she said, cheeks flushed with pride and shyness.

Sophie crouched, accepting the bouquet like the rarest treasure.

"Thank you, Emma. They're beautiful."

Emma bit her lip, glancing around as if to make sure no one overheard.

"You made it beautiful again," she whispered. "The square. My dad."

Sophie's throat tightened. She smoothed a stray lock of hair from Emma's face, touched by the quiet sincerity in her eyes.

"I didn't do it alone," Sophie said softly. "We all did."

But in that moment, holding the wildflowers, Sophie felt as if Marigold itself had placed them in her hands — not just as thanks, but as a sign: *You belong here.*

She straightened, Emma's small hand slipping into hers for just a second before the girl bounded away toward the fountain, where Cal was adjusting the last of the lights strung along the railings.

Sophie stood for a moment longer, breathing in the crisp, sweet air of a town on the brink of something new, the flowers in her arms and hope blooming in her heart.

The Square Comes Alive

By midmorning, the square had transformed into something that felt at once familiar and brand-new — as if the heart of Marigold had been waiting all these years for this exact moment to beat again.

Sophie stood at the edge of the square, bouquet of wildflowers still in her hands, watching as the pieces came together like a well-rehearsed dance.

The fountain, its stone cleaned and mended, sparkled in the sunlight. Water arched high, clear and sure, catching the light and tossing rainbows onto the brick below. Children gathered around it, daring each other closer, shrieking with laughter when a gust of wind sent spray across their faces.

The café buzzed with new life. Its windows gleamed, the doors propped open to let in the breeze and the music drifting from the bandstand. The jazz trio — a father, daughter, and son from two towns over — played a melody that felt stitched from sunlight and memory, easy and bright. The notes mingled with the scent of brewing coffee and warm cinnamon pastries, tempting passersby inside.

Food trucks lined the far edge of the square: one offering barbecue with smoke curling invitingly into the air, another dishing out tacos, their shells crisp and fragrant. A table of local bakers had set up near the bandstand, their goods laid out in neat rows: pies with golden crusts, cookies dusted with sugar, breads still warm from the oven.

Everywhere Sophie looked, there were signs of renewal.

The storefronts that only months ago had stood empty now displayed fresh paint, clean windows, and simple decorations: hand-lettered signs, planters overflowing with flowers, pennants strung across doorways.

The townspeople themselves seemed changed. Former skeptics — men and women who'd once crossed their arms and narrowed their eyes at Sophie's plans — now laughed with neighbors, their faces open and bright. Children ran free, weaving between tables and booths. Teenagers lounged against railings, pretending not to care but watching everything.

Even the air felt different — lighter, as if the weight Marigold had carried for so long had finally lifted.

Sophie moved through it all, offering smiles, lending a hand where needed, feeling the square's energy fill her.

At one point she paused beneath the bandstand, where the musicians hit their stride in a lilting tune that made people tap their feet and sway in place. A few couples danced — shyly at first, then with growing confidence, as if the music reminded them of who they'd been once, or who they still might be.

Jeanine approached, apron dusted with flour from the bake sale table, her smile wide and unguarded.

"You see this?" Jeanine said, voice warm. "This is what you brought back."

Sophie shook her head, heart full. "*We* brought it back."

Jeanine's gaze softened. "You gave us the reason. Don't forget that."

And Sophie didn't — not as she helped a boy untangle his kite string from a lamppost, or as she caught sight of Emma leading a pack of younger kids to the lemonade stand, or as Cal lifted a small child onto his shoulders to get a better view of the fountain.

Somewhere in the back of her mind, she knew the council's 30-day deadline still hung like a distant bell. The emergency promises — Cal's collateral offer, the patchwork pledges — had bought them breathing room, not guarantees. But for now, that didn't matter. Today was about the square, the people, the proof that something real had taken root.

The square wasn't just alive — it felt closer to whole.

And for the first time in a long time, Sophie felt like she was, too — though part of her knew the work wasn't finished. Not yet.

Cal's Speech

The band finished their set to a wave of applause, the last notes lingering in the summer air like a promise. The mayor stepped forward onto the bandstand, his suit slightly rumpled, his face flushed with heat or nerves — maybe both. He cleared his throat once, twice, then fumbled with his notecards.

"Uh, folks," he began, voice wavering, "I just want to say how, uh, proud we are — I mean, I am — of what's happened here today. Thanks to the hard work of many people, and, um, our community spirit, and, uh…"

The words trailed off as he shuffled the cards, struggling to find his place. A murmur rippled through the crowd — polite, but restless.

Then, without fanfare, Cal stepped forward.

Sophie hadn't seen him move. One moment he'd been standing beside Emma near the fountain, arms folded as he watched the proceedings. The next, he was climbing the bandstand steps, his boots ringing out on the old wood.

The mayor, relieved, stepped aside with a grateful nod.

Cal stood there for a beat, hands shoved into his back pockets, gazing out at the crowd. He didn't carry notes. He didn't need them.

"I wasn't planning to speak," he said, voice steady, carrying across the square with quiet strength. "Guess I figured I'd let the mayor handle it. But seeing as he looks like he'd rather be anywhere else right now…"

A ripple of laughter — light and genuine — broke the tension.

Cal's eyes swept the square.

"Look at this place," he said. "Just — look at it. I remember when this square was the heart of everything. Where my parents brought me for ice cream on Friday nights. Where I taught Emma to ride her bike. Where we had Christmas parades and summer fairs and every little memory that stitched this town together.

"And then one by one, we started losing it. The shops closed. The fountain dried up. Folks started leaving, or giving up, or just… stopped seeing it for what it was."

He paused, drawing a breath. The sunlight caught the silver threads at his temples, the lines carved deep at the corners of his eyes.

"And maybe some of us thought — me included — that it was too late to get it back. That Marigold had had its day. That hope was for fools."

Sophie felt her throat tighten.

Cal's gaze found hers, held it.

"But then someone showed up who saw what we'd stopped seeing. Someone who reminded us this square, this town, *us* — we're worth fighting for. Worth fixing. Worth believing in."

The crowd was silent now, drawn close by the honesty in his words.

"She didn't do it with speeches. Not really. She did it by showing up. By listening. By getting her hands dirty right alongside us. And she didn't do it alone, either. Every one of you — you're the reason this square looks the way it does today. You're the reason we've got music playing, and kids laughing, and hope where we thought there wasn't any left."

Cal swallowed, his voice dipping softer, more personal.

"I guess what I'm trying to say is — this isn't just about a fountain that runs again, or a café that reopened its doors — or the temporary funds we scraped together to make today happen. It's about what happens when we stop waiting for someone else to save the town and start saving it ourselves. Together. And this? This is just the beginning."

A beat. Then, applause — warm, full-throated and real. But beneath the pride, Sophie caught glimpses of uncertainty in a few faces — folks still wondering if hope could truly hold.

Cal stepped back, eyes never leaving Sophie's as the crowd cheered. And in that look was everything he didn't say: gratitude. Admiration. And maybe, just maybe, something more.

The Moment of Truth

The applause from Cal's speech echoed through the square like a heartbeat — steady, strong, alive. Sophie stood at the edge of the bandstand, hands clasped lightly before her, watching as neighbors clapped each other on the back, as kids tugged at parents' hands to get closer to the fountain.

She hadn't planned anything beyond today — no big unveilings, no grand gestures. She'd thought the square itself would speak louder than any speech. But as the crowd began to quiet, as all those expectant faces turned toward her, Sophie realized they were waiting.

Not for another promise. Not for another plan.

For closure. For connection.

Her pulse raced, but she stepped forward, drawn by something larger than fear.

"Thank you," she began, voice steady though her heart thudded hard. "For letting me be part of this. For letting me try."

She looked out over the square — the cleaned fountain, the repainted storefronts, the string lights swaying gently in the summer breeze. But it wasn't the bricks and mortar that filled her with awe. It was the people.

"When I came back to Marigold, I thought I was here to help fix the square. To bring it back to what it was. But the truth is — *you* brought it back. Every nail hammered. Every weed pulled. Every hour you gave when you could've been doing anything else. That's what made this happen."

Her throat tightened, but she pressed on, voice soft but clear.

"I didn't just find a project here. I found a home I didn't know I still had. And I want to thank you — all of you — for showing me that."

She reached down and lifted the covering cloth from a small plaque mounted at the base of the fountain. The brushed bronze gleamed in the afternoon sun.

The crowd edged closer, reading the inscription as she spoke it aloud.

"For the people of Marigold — past, present, and future — whose hands rebuilt what mattered."

A hush fell. For a moment, all that could be heard was the soft trickle of water from the fountain and the distant hum of cicadas.

Then the oldest man in town — Mr. Harper, who had once been the most vocal critic of Sophie's plans — cleared his throat. His cane tapped the brick as he stepped forward.

"She got that right," he said, voice rough with emotion. "And if you ask me, this town's lucky she didn't give up on us."

The silence broke like a wave against the shore. Applause rose again, but this time it was different — not polite, not hesitant, but full of pride, of ownership, of *belonging*.

Sophie exhaled, a tremor of relief and joy in her chest.

From the edge of the square, Cal caught her eye. His expression was unreadable at first — then softened, a slow, quiet smile breaking through. He gave a small nod, one hand resting lightly on Emma's shoulder.

It felt, Sophie thought, like a promise kept.

Sophie and Cal's Turning Point?

The sun dipped low, casting the square in that soft amber light that made everything — the brickwork, the fountain's spray, even the tired faces of the townsfolk — look burnished and beautiful. The festival was winding down. Laughter still echoed here and there, but families were packing up, vendors were closing shop, and the band was playing their final tune, slow and sweet.

Sophie stood near the fountain, watching as Emma chased fireflies with a pack of other kids, their giggles rising like song. The square was glowing — not just from the string lights, but from the spirit of it, alive in a way Sophie hadn't dared to hope.

"Looks good from up here too."

Cal's voice, low and warm, made her turn. He stood beside her, hands in his pockets, face softened by the glow of the lights.

She smiled, tired but full. "It does."

He tilted his head toward the far end of the square. "Come on. I want to show you something."

They walked together, weaving between the tables being folded up, the strings of lights swaying overhead. Cal led her to the edge of the square, where scaffolding still stood beside one of the buildings slated for final restoration.

Without a word, he climbed, sure and steady, and offered her a hand. Sophie hesitated only a second before taking it, the roughness of his palm grounding her.

They stood together at the top, overlooking the square. The view took her breath — the fountain gleaming, the shopfronts aglow, the people lingering as if unwilling to leave this reclaimed heart of their town.

"This is what I was afraid to hope for," Cal said quietly.

Sophie glanced at him. The guardedness was gone from his face, replaced by something raw and real.

"I thought if I let myself believe it could come back — that we could come back — I'd only end up watching it slip away again. Like I watched her slip away."

His meaning was clear without him saying more. His wife. His loss.

Sophie's heart ached for him, for all the ways he'd tried to hold this place together with his own two hands.

"I know that fear," she said softly. "Every plan I drew up, I kept wondering — am I doing this for Marigold? Or to make up for the fact I left? Or because I want to belong somewhere again, and I don't know how to ask for it?"

Cal turned, really looking at her now. The square faded around them — it was just the two of them, two people who'd fought so hard not just for a place, but for a piece of themselves.

"I'm glad you came back," he said, voice rough with truth. "Not for the square. For us. For Emma."

Sophie felt it then — that fragile, precious thing between them that had been building in stolen glances, in shared work, in arguments that meant they cared.

"I'm glad I did too," she said.

They stood like that, close but not quite touching, as the last of the festival sounds faded and the square settled into its new life.

And in that moment, Sophie realized they hadn't just rebuilt a town square. They'd begun to rebuild themselves.

Under the Lights

The square had quieted now. The last of the vendors had packed up, their laughter and goodbyes fading down Main Street. The bandstand stood empty, the echo of music lingering in the warm night air. The fountain's soft trickle was the only sound, mingling with the hum of cicadas and the occasional bark of a dog somewhere in the distance.

Sophie and Cal remained at the top of the scaffolding, bathed in the soft glow of the string lights that crisscrossed the square. The lights swayed gently in the breeze, casting a golden net over the town they had fought so hard to save.

Below, Emma danced barefoot with the other children, their shadows long and loose on the bricks. Fireflies blinked between the trees, tiny stars come to earth.

For a long moment, neither Sophie nor Cal spoke. They simply stood together, the shared silence richer than any words.

Cal's gaze found hers in the hush. "You did this," he said quietly.

"No," Sophie whispered. "*We* did."

His eyes softened, and the weight of everything — the sleepless

nights, the hard choices, the fights, the laughter, the tentative trust —
shimmered between them, as real as the lights above.

Cal shifted closer, not enough to touch, but enough that Sophie
could feel the heat of him, the steady grounding presence that had
become as much a part of this place as the bricks beneath their feet.

"You stayed," he said, almost like he couldn't believe it.

"I didn't want to," Sophie said, breath catching. "I needed to."

Cal's hand found hers just as a firework bloomed behind them,
casting light across the square. He pulled her in — not for a kiss, not
quite — but for a fierce, brief hug that spoke of everything they'd fought
for. When they drew back, their foreheads touched for a breathless
instant, the square and all its promise shining around them.

A cheer rose unexpectedly from below — Emma and the other
kids, catching sight of them on the scaffolding, clapping and laughing as
fireworks burst behind the trees.

Cal and Sophie pulled back, just enough to smile at each other.

"Well," Cal murmured, eyes crinkling at the corners, "guess we're
official now."

Sophie laughed, a sound full of relief and joy. "About time."

They stood there, watching as the fireworks painted the sky, the
square aglow with hope and light and the future they'd started to build
— together.

Where we belong

Night had fully claimed the square, but it wasn't dark. The string lights
glowed like low-hung stars, draping the square in warmth. The last of the
fireworks crackled in the distance, their smoke mingling with the faint
scent of roasted peanuts, fresh-cut grass, and the sharp tang of spent
sparklers.

Sophie and Cal had climbed down from the scaffolding, their
fingers brushing, their smiles quiet but full. They didn't need more words
right now. The square spoke for them.

Around them, Marigold lived again.

Children chased fireflies across the grass, their laughter rising and falling like song. Elderly couples swayed slowly to the fading notes of the band's last tune, their worn boots scuffing against the bricks. Teenagers leaned against lampposts, watching it all with that mix of boredom and wonder that comes when home suddenly feels special again.

Jeanine sat on the café's reopened patio, sipping sweet tea, her face soft with pride as she watched her neighbors reclaim the night. At the fountain, a boy and girl tossed in coins, making whispered wishes that felt sacred in the hush.

The fountain itself shimmered under the lights, the water catching gold and silver threads of reflection. It seemed, in that moment, not just restored, but reborn — a promise in stone and water that this place, these people, would endure.

Sophie stood at its edge, hand still lightly in Cal's, and let the moment fill her. She saw it all: the square as it was, as it had been, as it could be. And for the first time, she didn't feel like a stranger standing at the edge of it.

Cal turned slightly, brushing a lock of hair from her cheek. "Feels different now," he said softly.

"It *is* different now," Sophie replied.

Emma raced toward them then, breathless from chasing fireflies. She grabbed Sophie's hand and Cal's, linking them together. "Come see!" she urged. "Come see the lanterns by the creek!"

And so they went — the three of them — through the square, past the tables and benches they'd repaired, past the shops that now glowed with new hope, past the fountain that sang again.

Neighbors called out goodnights. Someone strummed a guitar near the old bandstand. The square hummed, alive, no longer a place of memories alone, but of *possibility*.

As they reached the edge of the square, Sophie glanced back one last time. The view etched itself into her heart: a town not healed, not perfect, but rising.

A place where she belonged. A place where they all did.

Chapter 11

The Promise of Tomorrow

The first light of day seeped through the gauzy curtains of Sophie's new home — not the polished inn room where she'd first stayed, but the creaky old house at the edge of the square she'd chosen to make her own. It had once belonged to a milliner, the town's records said, though time had long since stolen the trace of hats or ribbons. Now, it was hers — or would be, once the endless repairs were done. The porch sagged slightly on the east side. The paint peeled in soft curls along the window frames. But it was hers.

Sophie sat on the porch steps, a chipped mug of coffee cradled between her palms, watching as Marigold woke around her. A cat — she'd learned its name was Tilly, though it seemed to belong to no one — slinked across the square, pausing to sniff at the base of the newly replanted flowerbeds. The fountain bubbled steadily, its steady trickle a music she'd come to love. Sunlight glinted on the water, catching the arc of a single stream as it fell into the basin.

The square hummed, soft and low at this hour. A delivery truck rattled past, stopping at the café where Hester could be seen setting out chairs, her apron already dusted with flour. The shopkeepers rolled up their metal gates one by one, as if revealing the town's heart in slow motion. The scent of bread, earth, and something faintly floral — maybe the crepe myrtle just beginning to bloom — carried on the breeze. A soundscape of small-town life: a child's laughter from somewhere unseen, the rhythmic thwack of a broom on brick, the lazy creak of a sign swaying on its hook.

Sophie closed her eyes for a moment, letting it all wash over her. This was what they'd fought for. What she'd fought for. Not just the buildings scrubbed clean or the square free of weeds — but this quiet, ordinary morning. A place where people lingered, where laughter mingled with work, where hope lived in small, steady ways.

Her gaze drifted to the corner where Cal's workshop sat, the doors still closed at this hour. But she knew he'd be there soon — he always was, early and steady as sunrise. The thought warmed her. What had begun as tension, friction, had become something else entirely. She couldn't name it yet, not fully. But it filled the quiet spaces between them, like light finding its way through cracked shutters.

She drew in a long breath, tasting the coffee's bitterness and the morning's sweetness both. The house behind her still smelled faintly of paint and sawdust, a work in progress. Just like her. Just like Marigold.

Then came the sound of small feet on the path — and Sophie turned, already smiling.

Cal and Emma Join

The clatter of bicycle tires on the brick path broke the quiet rhythm of Sophie's thoughts. She glanced up, shielding her eyes against the rising sun, and spotted Emma pedaling toward her, Cal walking alongside at an easy pace, one hand resting lightly on the handlebars to steady the wobbly front wheel.

Emma hopped off before the bike fully stopped, breathless and flushed with pride. She wore a faded t-shirt that boasted *Marigold Elementary Field Day 2017* in peeling letters, and a pair of jean shorts frayed at the hem. In her arms she cradled a bundle of wildflowers — bright, uneven, glorious — clearly picked along the edge of town.

"For your porch," she said, thrusting the flowers toward Sophie with the wide-eyed earnestness only a child could offer. "Daddy says it needs a little color."

Sophie accepted them, touched in a way she hadn't expected. The stems were uneven, some bent, some broken, but the colors sang against the chipped paint of the steps — yellows and purples, a single red poppy that leaned at a crooked angle. "They're perfect," she said softly. "Thank you, Emma."

Cal reached them, a small smile playing at his lips. He carried a clay pot in one hand — a planter, plain but sturdy, the kind that promised to last through seasons of sun and rain. Without a word, he set it down beside Sophie's coffee mug. "Figured the steps could use this too," he said. His voice was easy, the tension that once shadowed every interaction now softened into something gentler.

Sophie knelt, arranging the flowers into the pot, fingers brushing soil, arranging stems, feeling the morning's peace settle into her bones. She glanced up at Cal, catching him watching her — not with the wary skepticism of those early days, but with something closer to quiet wonder. She felt warmth rise to her cheeks, unexpected and welcome.

Emma plopped down beside Sophie, swinging her legs over the edge of the porch. "Guess what?" she said, nearly bursting with excitement. "Mrs. Jenkins picked me to help design the mural for the community center! She said my drawing of the square gave her the idea!"

Sophie blinked, then grinned, genuinely thrilled. "Emma, that's amazing. I can't wait to see what you create."

"She wants it to show what Marigold was and what it is now," Emma went on, voice tumbling over itself in excitement. "And what it could be. Like, a before and after, but together."

Cal crouched down, ruffling his daughter's hair. "Told you that drawing of yours was special."

Emma leaned against his side, and Sophie's heart squeezed at the sight — the easy closeness, the way Cal's rough exterior melted in his daughter's presence. And for just a moment, Sophie let herself picture it — not just the square restored, but this: quiet mornings, shared plans, laughter that echoed off newly painted walls.

"Maybe you could help me sketch it?" Emma asked, hopeful.

"I'd be honored," Sophie said. And she meant it.

They sat like that for a few moments longer — Sophie, Cal, and Emma — watching the square come alive around them. The square wasn't perfect yet. Neither were they. But something good had taken root, and Sophie felt it grow stronger with every shared morning.

A Small Celebration

The sun climbed higher, casting soft gold across the square as the trio made their way down Main Street. The morning bustle had fully begun now, and with it came the small, everyday magic Sophie had fought so hard to help restore.

Shop doors stood propped open, letting out scents of fresh bread and coffee. Wind chimes sang from the hardware store awning, their tune mingling with the low hum of conversation and the occasional bark of a dog.

Neighbors waved as Sophie, Cal, and Emma passed. Some offered cautious nods, others warm greetings that spoke of bridges mended. At the corner, Mrs. Dawkins — long one of Sophie's harshest critics — lifted a hand in acknowledgment, her face softening just enough to show she, too, had begun to see Sophie differently.

They paused outside Marigold Books & History, where Jeanine stood on a small stepstool adjusting the display window. She spotted them and grinned, a rare full grin that crinkled the corners of her sharp eyes. "You three look like a postcard," she called. "Missing only a dog."

Emma giggled, glancing up at Cal with a mischievous glint. "Told you we need one, Daddy."

Cal groaned, but there was no heat behind it. "Don't encourage her, Jeanine."

Sophie felt the warmth of belonging bloom in her chest — unexpected, profound. This was no grand festival, no orchestrated event. It was smaller than that. Quieter. But it was a celebration just the same: of community, of connection, of the simple joy of walking through a place that no longer looked at her as a stranger.

Hester Boyd emerged from the café, wiping her hands on a gingham towel. She nodded to Sophie, an approving glint in her eye that hadn't been there months ago. "Morning," she said. "The usual's on the house today. Call it a thank you for stubbornness well-placed."

Sophie accepted the coffee gratefully, touched by the small but genuine gesture. "That means more than you know, Hester."

Cal handed Emma a napkin-wrapped muffin from the tray by the counter. The girl beamed as she bit into it, crumbs dusting her chin.

Together, they wandered through the square — not in a rush, not with any agenda. Just walking, greeting, taking it all in. Sophie noticed the little things: fresh paint on a windowsill, a new flowerpot outside the barber shop, the way people lingered longer on benches, chatting rather than passing through.

They passed the fountain, still flowing steadily, its soft burble like music beneath the town's gentle murmur. Emma skipped ahead to toss in a penny, closing her eyes tight as she made her wish.

"What do you think she wished for?" Sophie asked quietly, watching Cal watch his daughter.

He smiled, a real one, soft at the edges. "Knowing Emma? A puppy. Or maybe that the ice cream shop brings back the bubblegum flavor."

Sophie laughed, and the sound felt easy, right. "Both worthy wishes."

The morning stretched, unhurried, stitched together with small kindnesses and shared glances. It wasn't a grand celebration. But as they passed neighbor after neighbor — as shopkeepers tipped their hats and children waved — Sophie realized this was the sweetest kind of victory. The kind you earned slowly, through trust built one small act at a time.

The midday sun slanted through the café's wide front windows, casting soft light across the worn wooden table where Sophie, Cal, and Emma had settled. Outside, the square pulsed with quiet life: the clink of dishes from the café patio, the low hum of conversation, the steady rhythm of a carpenter's hammer somewhere down the block.

Emma sat cross-legged on her chair, absorbed in her muffin, while Sophie sipped her coffee, feeling both the warmth of the mug and of the day itself settle into her bones. It was the first time in months she wasn't thinking about what needed fixing. She was simply *here* — in a place that finally felt like hers.

Cal reached into the satchel he'd slung over the chair back and pulled out a rolled sheaf of papers secured with a worn leather tie. He laid them on the table between them, the crackle of old blueprints breaking the comfortable quiet.

Sophie raised a brow, intrigued. "What's this?"

Cal's lips quirked into the smallest of smiles. "An idea. Been rattling around in my head longer than I care to admit."

He untied the roll and spread the papers out. The lines were faded, the margins smudged with years of handling. But Sophie saw at once the bones of something special: the outline of the old warehouse on the edge of town, reimagined as something more.

"A community arts and learning center," Cal said, his voice low, almost tentative. "Place for kids to paint, build, play. Rooms for workshops, reading corners, maybe even a little stage for music or plays. I used to think about it when Emma was small. Never could make it work. But now… with what we've done here…"

Sophie's heart tightened at the hope woven through his words, at the rare vulnerability in his eyes. She traced a finger along one of the sketch's lines — a sun-filled courtyard, a mural wall, space for gardens and picnic tables.

"This is beautiful," she said softly. "And doable. We can build this,

Cal. The town would rally behind it."

Emma leaned over the plans, wide-eyed. "Could there be a space for dogs?" she asked hopefully.

Cal chuckled, ruffling her hair. "You and those dogs."

Sophie grinned. "I'm sure we can work a dog park into the design."

Without thinking, she grabbed a napkin and a pen from her bag, sketching quick ideas: awnings here, solar panels there, rainwater collection along the sides. Cal watched her, the admiration in his gaze unguarded now.

They bent over the plans together, napkin and blueprint side by side, heads nearly touching as they swapped ideas, their voices low and easy. The café around them faded, the square beyond becoming a backdrop for the future they were sketching with ink and imagination.

Laughter bubbled between them as Cal teased Sophie's hasty doodles — "That looks like a chicken coop, not a tool shed" — and Sophie countered with mock indignation. Emma offered earnest suggestions, her excitement infectious.

By the time the coffee was cold and the muffin crumbs long gone, the napkin was covered in notes and drawings. Sophie leaned back, realizing her cheeks ached from smiling.

"This feels good," she said, her voice laced with quiet wonder. "To dream beyond the square. To imagine what comes next."

Cal nodded, his gaze steady on hers. "We've come this far. Might as well keep going. Maybe this is how we keep the momentum alive — build on it, literally."

There was a warmth in his words that wasn't just about the project. It was about them. About the quiet partnership taking root between blueprints and shared hopes.

Outside, the fountain's gentle splash mingled with the sound of children's laughter, the square alive with the promise of what could be.

A Shared Vow

The day lingered long and golden as afternoon faded toward evening.

The square, for all its quiet bustle earlier, had settled into a soft hum — the kind of peace that comes when a town exhales after a good day's work.

Sophie and Cal found themselves at the fountain's edge, as if drawn there by instinct. The water caught the late sun's glow, scattering patterns of light across their faces. A breeze lifted strands of Sophie's hair, and she didn't bother to tame them; it felt right to let the moment be unpolished, real.

They sat side by side on the cool stone, shoulders almost touching, watching Emma race after a butterfly near the café's patio, her laughter carrying across the square like music.

For a long while, neither spoke. There was no need. The silence felt full rather than empty, as if the square itself was part of the conversation.

Finally, Cal cleared his throat, voice low. "I used to think this place was beyond saving," he admitted. His gaze stayed fixed on the water, as if it was easier to confess to the fountain than to Sophie. "Thought maybe it was foolish to keep trying. But you — you didn't just bring plans or blueprints. You brought… belief. And that made the rest of us start to believe, too."

Sophie felt a lump rise in her throat, unexpected and overwhelming. She blinked it back, searching for words that wouldn't sound trite or rehearsed.

"I didn't do this alone," she said quietly. "And I don't want to. Not now. Not ever."

Cal turned to look at her then, really look, the weight of everything unspoken in his eyes — gratitude, relief, something deeper and warmer that neither of them dared name just yet.

"I'm in this," he said, the words simple but steady. "For the square. For the town. For you. I want to keep building. Whatever comes next… I want us to face it together."

Sophie drew in a slow breath, letting the promise settle between them like stone laid sure and strong. She glanced down at the plaque on the fountain, the one she'd agonized over the night before the grand reopening. *For the people of Marigold — past, present, and future — whose hands rebuilt what mattered.*

The words felt fuller now. Truer.

She reached out, her fingers brushing Cal's — just a touch, but enough. "Together," she echoed, and meant it.

And in that simple word, Sophie felt a tremor of something larger than the square, larger than the day's victories. She felt the shape of a life she hadn't dared to imagine — Cal's hand steady beneath hers, Emma's laughter threading through the dusk, a place at the heart of it all where she might belong. Her heart beat stronger, not with certainty, but with the fragile, thrilling hope that this could be more than rebuilding a town. This could be rebuilding a home. A family. Maybe even herself.

And as she sat there, the weight of that wondering filled her — tender, tentative, but real — and she let herself want it.

They sat like that as the sky shifted from gold to rose to lavender. The square belonged to them in that moment — not as a possession, but as a shared promise. A foundation laid not just of brick and mortar, but of trust, of hope, of the quiet strength that comes from choosing to stay, to build, to believe.

Emma's voice broke the spell, sweet and insistent. "Look! Fireflies!" She darted toward the garden beds where the tiny lights had begun to dance in the dusk.

Cal chuckled, the sound warm and unguarded. "Guess it's that time."

Sophie smiled, heart full. "It's a good time."

And as the first stars pricked the sky above Marigold, they stayed at the fountain's edge — two souls who had found, at last, not just a place to begin… but someone to begin it with.

A place to begin

The sky above Marigold deepened from lavender to indigo, the last blush of sunset fading behind the hills. The square glowed in the gentle light of lanterns strung between lampposts, their soft halos casting warmth over cobblestones and storefronts. The fountain's steady trickle mingled with the low murmur of evening: a neighbor's quiet greeting, the clink of dishes being cleared from the café, the rustle of wind through the crepe myrtles.

Sophie sat on the fountain's rim, leaning lightly into Cal's side, content in the quiet. His arm wasn't around her, not yet, but the closeness between them was as sure and steady as the water that flowed beside them.

Emma chased fireflies near the garden plots, her laughter ringing out as she cupped her hands around one and held it close, its tiny light flickering between her fingers. She ran back to them, cheeks flushed, eyes bright with the wonder only childhood can hold.

"Look!" she said, opening her hands just enough to show the captured glow. "I caught one!"

Sophie bent forward, peering into Emma's hands. "That's magic, right there," she whispered.

Emma grinned, then gently let the firefly go. They watched it drift upward, its light winking like a star just out of reach.

Cal exhaled slowly, the tension that had lived in his shoulders for so long finally, truly beginning to ease. "I didn't think we'd get here," he said, voice low, meant only for Sophie's ears. "Not really."

Sophie tilted her head, resting it briefly against his shoulder. "Neither did I," she admitted. "But I'm glad we were wrong."

They stayed that way as the square came alive in a way it hadn't in years. Music floated from a porch radio, blending with the soft splash of the fountain. Children darted between pools of lamplight, their shadows stretching and shrinking on the bricks. Couples strolled hand in hand, pausing to admire the fresh paint, the blooms in the planters, the small signs that said: *This place matters. We matter.*

Sophie let her gaze wander — to the bookstore's front window where Jeanine worked late by lamplight, to the café where Hester polished glasses behind the bar, to the hardware store where someone had propped open the door to let in the night breeze. Each detail stitched together the picture of a town not just surviving but beginning again.

And at the heart of it all stood the fountain, its water catching the lantern glow, its plaque glinting softly in the light: *For the people of Marigold — past, present, and future — whose hands rebuilt what mattered.* Sophie traced the words in her mind, feeling their truth settle in her bones.

Cal shifted slightly, so that their shoulders pressed together, solid and sure. "It's home now," he said simply.

Sophie smiled, the kind of smile that starts small but fills a person from the inside out. "It is."

Above them, the first stars broke through the dusk. Around them, Marigold exhaled — not the breath of relief, but of hope.

And as the night deepened, Sophie, Cal, and Emma stayed where they were, part of the square, part of the promise — part of what came next, whatever challenges it might bring.

Chapter 12

Lines in the Sand

The morning air was thick with humidity and tension. Sophie felt it the moment she stepped onto Main Street, the usual rhythm of shopkeepers opening their doors and neighbors exchanging greetings muted beneath the weight of something new — something unwelcome.

A folded copy of *The Marigold Gazette* lay abandoned on a bench outside the café, headlines bold and bruising:

ATLANTA FIRM UNVEILS BOLD PLAN: JOBS, GROWTH, AND A NEW FUTURE FOR MARIGOLD

Beside it, an artist's rendering spanned half the front page — sleek glass buildings where historic facades once stood, wide concrete plazas replacing cobblestone streets, the square's fountain erased entirely. In its place: a polished sculpture that looked as if it belonged in an airport, not in the heart of a small town.

Sophie's stomach knotted. She grabbed the paper, scanning the article. The promises leapt off the page: hundreds of jobs, tax incentives, immediate construction. Quotes from council members filled the column — some cautious, some already sounding convinced. And the final gut punch — the developer had secured preliminary support from two major property owners, ones Sophie had hoped would hold the line.

An emergency town meeting was already scheduled for that evening.

As she crossed the square, she caught sight of Councilwoman Hester Boyd exiting the hardware store, the older woman's face lined with worry. Their eyes met, and for the first time since Sophie had returned, Hester didn't offer her usual nod of encouragement.

Instead, she approached, voice low. "We have to consider all options, Sophie. People are scared. And desperate men make tempting offers." The words weren't cruel — just heavy with truth.

Sophie opened her mouth to argue, to plead — but found she had no breath, no words. The rendering burned in her mind — Marigold stripped of its soul, its past buried beneath steel and glass.

The square that had begun to feel like home suddenly felt fragile. Breakable.

Sophie's Crisis of Confidence

The door to her own house creaked as Sophie pushed it open, the faint scent of paint and sawdust greeting her — the smell of work unfinished, but hers. She hadn't planned to come home yet — not today. But after the paper's headlines and Hester's measured words, she'd needed the one place that still felt like hers. A place that reminded her what she was fighting for.

Dust motes floated in the warm light slanting through the parlor windows. Sophie sank onto the threadbare sofa, the same one where her mother had read to her on rainy afternoons, and dropped the *Gazette* onto the coffee table as if it might burn her fingers. The rendering on its front page stared back — that soulless sculpture, the square erased.

She buried her face in her hands.

For the first time since arriving in Marigold, the fight felt unwinnable. Every late night pouring over budgets, every delicate conversation with business owners, every hard-earned inch of trust — it all felt as fragile as the cracked porcelain vase on the mantel. One more blow and it would shatter.

Her gaze drifted to the mantel. The photo was still there — her mother in her garden, straw hat tilted back, grinning as if the world were a place worth believing in. Sophie reached for it, thumb tracing the familiar lines of that smile.

Her mother's voice echoed in memory, soft but certain:

"If you ever wonder what's worth fighting for, Sophie, look at what you'd miss if it were gone."

Sophie's throat tightened. She looked out the window, past the overgrown yard to where the square lay hidden beyond the trees. She pictured it — the fountain dry but waiting, the worn benches, the shopfronts that still dreamed of light behind their dusty panes.

Could she really walk away? Leave Marigold to the highest bidder? The thought made her ache in a place deeper than pride, deeper than ambition.

But fear whispered back: *What if you're wrong? What if you're just another outsider making promises you can't keep?*

She closed her eyes, the room silent but for the creak of the house settling around her, as if it too were bracing for the storm ahead.

And for the first time, the idea of giving up didn't just cross her mind — it stayed.

Cal's Choice

The knock was soft at first. Hesitant, almost as if whoever stood on the porch was second-guessing being there at all.

Sophie didn't move. The photo frame still rested in her lap, her thumb tracing the edge over and over, as if doing so might summon an answer. Another knock — firmer this time.

"Sophie? It's Cal."

His voice — rough around the edges, quieter than usual — filtered through the screen door like a memory she hadn't expected to need.

For a heartbeat, she considered not answering. Letting him think she'd gone for a walk, or was too tired, or too angry, or too broken to face him. But something in his tone — that unfamiliar gentleness — pulled her to her feet.

She opened the door. He stood there, hands shoved deep into his pockets, shoulders slightly hunched as if carrying the weight of his own doubts. The dying sun painted him in gold and rose, softening the lines of his face. For the first time in days, there was no defensiveness between them — only concern.

"I saw your car out front," he said. "Figured you might need—" He broke off, looking at her, really looking. "Well. I don't know what I figured. Just... needed to see how you were holding up."

Sophie stepped aside, and he entered, his boots quiet on the worn wooden floor. The room seemed smaller with him in it, the air thicker somehow.

"I'm not sure I am," Sophie admitted, voice low. "Holding up."

Cal nodded, glancing around at the old photographs, the sagging shelves. "I get it. The town's scared, Sophie. Scared folks cling to what looks like certainty — even if it's the wrong thing. Big promises are easier to believe when you're desperate."

Sophie's eyes stung. "What if I'm wrong, Cal? What if they're right to doubt me?"

Cal leaned against the doorway, arms folded, gaze steady but softer than she'd ever seen it. "I don't think you are. But that doesn't matter as much right now." He hesitated, then took a breath. "I've been asking myself something all morning. Figured it's time I asked you: What do you want? Not for Marigold. Not for the square. For you."

The question hit like a stone dropped into still water, rippling through everything she thought she knew.

"I... I want to matter," Sophie said at last. "I want to do something that lasts. Something that isn't just plans on paper. And I want this — this town — to feel like home again. I thought I could help it heal, and maybe I could heal something in me too."

For a long moment, Cal said nothing. Then he pushed away from the doorway and crossed the room, stopping just shy of touching her. His voice was low, rough with unspoken things. "You do matter. And you've done more than you see. But if you're staying in this fight... I'm with you. If you're not? Tell me now."

Sophie met his gaze. The tension between them hummed like a live wire — fear, hope, something more. And in that fragile space, they stopped being adversaries. They were just two people, standing at the edge of everything that could be lost — or built.

Emotional Climax

The room seemed to shrink around them — just Sophie and Cal, the soft creak of the old house settling, and the faint rhythm of their breathing filling the quiet.

Outside, the first stars pricked through the twilight, but neither noticed. Their focus was on each other, on the fragile thread stretched taut between them.

Sophie's heart pounded so hard she was sure he could hear it. Cal stood close enough that she could see the faint scar above his eyebrow, the line of wear at the collar of his flannel shirt, the way his hand twitched at his side like he didn't trust it not to reach for her.

"I'm not running," she said again, firmer this time. The words steadied her. "Not from this. Not from you. Not anymore."

Something flickered in Cal's eyes — relief, maybe, or the dangerous hope he'd been trying to tamp down for too long. He lifted a hand, slowly, as if giving her the chance to pull away. His knuckles brushed her cheek, the barest whisper of contact, but it sent a jolt through her all the same. His thumb lingered for a breath, tracing an invisible line just beneath her eye, where tears had threatened but not fallen.

And then the moment shifted. The air between them thickened, charged. Cal's gaze dropped to her mouth. Sophie felt herself lean in, drawn by gravity stronger than reason. Their faces were so close now that she could feel the warmth of his breath, taste the coffee and worry that lingered there.

His hand moved, cupping her face fully, and she thought — *this is it.* The line they'd been dancing along for weeks would finally be crossed.

But Cal froze. His eyes searched hers, raw and wide, as if he were trying to memorize everything about her in this instant. Then, with visible effort, he stepped back, hand falling away, leaving her skin cold where he'd touched it.

"Sophie..." His voice was hoarse. "If I kiss you right now, I don't think I'll be able to stop wanting more. And I can't — I can't let this get tangled up in everything else unless we're sure. Unless you're sure."

Her breath hitched. The ache was sharp, but so was the tenderness behind his restraint. He wasn't pulling back because he didn't want her — he was pulling back because he did. Because it mattered.

"I am sure," she said, the words soft but certain. "But not tonight. Not like this. We finish the fight first."

Cal nodded, swallowing hard. "Then we finish it. Together."

Outside, the wind stirred the trees, and from somewhere down the block came the sound of a screen door banging shut — the town settling in for the night, unaware of the promise just made in that quiet room.

The storm broke after midnight.

Wind rattled the windows, and rain lashed against the glass. Sophie sat at the small kitchen table, a mug of untouched tea cooling beside her. Sleep felt as far away as the stars hidden beyond the clouds. Through the rain-slicked window, the square was a blur of wet lamplight and dark shapes. Even the fountain, so solid by day, seemed uncertain in the storm.

Her phone buzzed, startling her in the quiet. She hesitated, dread prickling the back of her neck before she even saw the screen.

Nathan.

For a moment she just stared at the name, the letters blurring as the storm pressed against the glass. The city felt a lifetime away — but his name pulled it all back. The late nights at his apartment, the plans made and broken, the love that had once felt inevitable until it wasn't.

She answered.

"Sophie," Nathan said, his voice warm and familiar and achingly distant all at once. "I—I hope it's not too late."

"It's late," she said, softer than she meant to. "And raining."

A beat of silence. The storm filled it, wind howling through the eaves.

"I couldn't stop thinking about you tonight," Nathan said. "I thought—God, I thought maybe I'd come up, see you. Maybe I made a mistake, letting you go."

Her chest tightened. Outside, lightning lit the square for a heartbeat — the fountain, the scaffolding, the banner that had come loose and flapped wildly in the wind.

"Nathan…" she began, but the words tangled. Part of her wanted to cling to the familiar, to the version of herself who had belonged in his world. But that Sophie had left, hadn't she? She'd walked away. She'd chosen this place, this fight. And maybe, maybe she was choosing something — someone — else too.

"I should go," Nathan said, his voice low. "I shouldn't have called. I'm sorry."

"Nathan, wait—" But the line was already dead.

Sophie lowered the phone, her hand trembling. The storm raged on, but inside her, the storm was quieter now. Not gone. But clearer. She knew what she had to let go of — and what she wasn't ready to lose.

In the morning, Marigold would still be there. The square. The fight. And maybe, if she dared, Cal.

A Plan Takes Shape

The quiet that settled between them after that near-kiss wasn't empty. It was filled with something new — resolve, trust, the fragile beginnings of *us.* They didn't say it, but both felt it. The air no longer crackled with only tension; now it hummed with shared purpose.

Sophie exhaled slowly, gathering herself. She crossed to the table where the blueprints were unrolled, their edges curling, the paper smudged with coffee rings and fingerprints from weeks of hard work. Cal joined her, his presence steady at her side. The warmth of him calmed her racing thoughts.

"We need something big," Sophie said, voice low but gaining strength. "Something that reminds them what we're fighting for — and why it's worth the risk."

Cal leaned over the plans, his finger tracing the outline of the square. "The town's scared. The developer's offering security — or at least the illusion of it. We can't match their money. But we can show heart. We can show what we're made of."

Sophie nodded. "What if we stop *telling* them and start *showing* them? A day where the town sees what this place could be — not on paper, but for real. Music, food, community booths, a mock-up of the restored storefronts. We clean up what we can. We light it up — literally and figuratively."

Cal's brows rose, a grin tugging at the corner of his mouth despite the weight of the moment. "A Square Revival Day."

She grinned back. "Exactly."

He rubbed the back of his neck, thinking. "We can rally the tradesfolk. The café' will donate coffee, I'll bet. Jeanine can set up something with the historical society — old photos, maybe a storytelling tent. We'll need supplies."

"I'll cover what I can," Sophie said. "And I'll reach out to my contacts — maybe we can get in-kind donations for things like lights and paint."

They began sketching ideas on scrap paper, napkins, the margins of the blueprints — a flurry of motion and energy. The weariness of the long day fell away as excitement took its place. They scribbled lists:

volunteers to call, supplies to gather, permits to request. Sophie's pen raced as fast as her pulse.

Cal paused, watching her. "You know this won't be easy. People are going to test us at every turn."

"I'm done being afraid of that," Sophie said, meeting his gaze. "We let them see our hearts. If that's not enough, at least we'll know we gave it everything."

"And maybe," Cal added, "this buys us more time — even if it's a stopgap. The thirty-day window's still hanging over us."

Sophie nodded, sobering. "It may never come to that. But we treat it like it might."

His voice softened. "Then let's do it."

The night grew deeper outside, the moon rising over the square. But in that small room — crowded with plans and possibility — a new light had ignited. Together, they'd drawn a line in the sand. And together, they would see it through.

The Spark of Hope

The first faint blush of dawn streaked the horizon, painting the edges of Marigold's rooftops in rose and gold. The square, silent for so long, seemed to hold its breath, waiting for the day to decide its fate. Sophie stood at the center of it all, arms folded, blueprint scraps still clutched in one hand. She hadn't slept — not really. The adrenaline of the plan they'd mapped out, the weight of what lay ahead, had kept her wired through the night.

Her boots crunched softly on the brickwork as she paced a slow circle around the fountain. The water was still, the stone rim cool beneath her fingertips when she paused to touch it. *This is where it starts*, she thought. *Or ends*. But for the first time, that thought didn't feel like surrender. It felt like a promise.

A creak of a door broke the quiet. Sophie turned, startled, to see the bookstore's front door swinging open. Jeanine stepped out, cardigan pulled tight against the morning chill, a steaming mug in hand. Without a word, she crossed to Sophie, offered the mug — tea, from the smell of it — and stood beside her, shoulder to shoulder. The silence between them wasn't awkward. It was companionable, steady.

"You really didn't sleep?" Jeanine finally asked, voice low.

Sophie shook her head, managing a tired smile. "Didn't feel like I could. Too much to do. Too much to lose."

Jeanine sipped from her own mug. "You've already done more than most would."

Sophie looked away, throat tight. "Not enough yet."

The sound of footsteps echoed faintly down Main Street. Sophie turned again — this time to see a small figure hurrying toward the square, ponytail bobbing, oversized backpack slung across one shoulder. Emma. Breathless, cheeks pink from the brisk air, determination bright in her eyes.

"I couldn't sleep either," Emma said by way of greeting. "Daddy's still at the shop getting his tools, but I wanted to be first." She dropped her bag and pulled out a sketchbook, flipping to a fresh page. "I'm gonna draw the square today. What it looks like now. And then later, what it looks like after."

Sophie blinked back the sudden sting of tears. The square wasn't empty anymore. It was filling — with hope, with action, with people who believed.

From the other end of the street came more signs of life: the rattle of a cart as the café owner wheeled out folding chairs; the soft clang of tools as Cal and his crew rounded the corner, sleeves rolled, ready to work. The morning light caught Cal's face just as he spotted her — and in his nod, in the faint smile that curved his lips, Sophie felt the first true flicker of confidence that this plan, this dream, might just take root.

She straightened, drawing in a deep breath of the crisp air, the scent of coffee and woodsmoke mingling as the town began to stir. The battle wasn't over — far from it. But she wasn't alone anymore. And that made all the difference.

Chapter 13

Square Revival Day

The first light of morning broke soft and silver, casting the square in a fragile glow that made the cracked bricks and weary storefronts look almost new. Sophie stood at her window, the curtain pushed aside, coffee cooling in her hands. For a moment, she let herself simply watch — the square she had fought for, still and waiting, like a stage before the play begins.

Her heart thudded with a mix of nerves and hope. This day mattered. Not because it was perfect — it wouldn't be. But because it was real — action, not promises.

She dressed quickly: jeans, boots sturdy enough for hauling supplies, a worn work shirt she hadn't planned to pack but was grateful to have. The mirror caught her face as she passed. Tired, yes. But determined. And beneath the weariness, a flicker of excitement — the kind that came with possibility.

When she stepped onto the square, the morning chill nipped at her cheeks. The air smelled of dew and old stone. The square was quiet, but not empty.

Jeanine was there already, a wool shawl draped over her shoulders, setting up a folding table near the fountain. She worked without fuss, arranging yellowing photographs in mismatched frames, unrolling maps that curled stubbornly at the edges. Sophie approached, hands shoved into her pockets.

"You didn't have to come this early," Sophie said.

Jeanine glanced up, eyes twinkling. "Didn't want to miss the start of something worth remembering." She gestured to a battered sign she'd propped against the table: *Marigold — Then & Now*. "Figured folks need reminding where we started before they can see where we're going."

Sophie swallowed the lump rising in her throat and nodded.

Further down the square, two teenagers — kids Sophie barely recognized from cleanup days — worked together to hang a banner between two lampposts. The painted letters weren't perfect; the R in *Rising* sagged a little, but the spirit was there: *Marigold Rising*. The banner swayed gently in the breeze, and Sophie felt the first true lift of hope in her chest.

Hester Boyd emerged from the café, balancing a tray of paper cups. She set up a makeshift station on the stoop and called out, "Coffee's on the house today! Builders drink free!" Her grin — rare and genuine — melted the usual reserve she wore like an apron.

Then came the sound Sophie had been straining for: the low rumble of a truck, the clatter of a trailer hitch, the scrape of toolboxes hitting the ground. Cal. He and his crew fanned out wordlessly, hauling ladders, sawhorses, buckets of paint. Cal met Sophie's eyes across the square and tipped his chin in greeting. No need for words — not yet. They were here, ready.

The square felt different now. No longer waiting. Becoming.

Sophie drew a long breath, the cool air filling her lungs. *Let's begin.*

The Square Comes Alive

The square, so long silent except for the sigh of the wind or the lonely creak of a loose signboard, now filled with the sounds of life. Hammers tapping, shovels scraping, voices calling directions — the symphony of work. It started in small ripples: a broom sweeping grit from the fountain's edge, a ladder propped against a warped lamppost, a wheelbarrow rattling over uneven bricks. But soon, the ripples overlapped, and the square was awash in motion.

Sophie moved through it all like a conductor without a baton — sleeves rolled, clipboard forgotten somewhere, her hands as dusty as any laborer's. A group of kids, faces smudged with dirt and determination, repainted a bench in bold green strokes. The paint dripped, the lines weren't neat, but the bench had never looked prouder.

She paused to watch as two elderly brothers, retired carpenters who'd once built half the town's porches, took turns power-washing the brick of a long-abandoned storefront. The red beneath the grime glowed like memory made visible. One of them caught Sophie's eye and gave a short nod — not exactly approval, but acceptance. It meant the world.

Local teens hauled sacks of soil to the planters that lined the square. With Jeanine's guidance, they tucked herbs and bright flowers into the dirt, their laughter mixing with the warm scent of basil and marigold blooms. A small girl, no more than five, solemnly watered each plant with a plastic cup, the water sloshing over her sneakers. Her mother watched nearby, smiling through tears she didn't bother to hide.

In one of the empty shop windows, volunteers taped up a display: black-and-white photos of the square in its prime alongside Sophie's colorful renderings of what could be. People stopped, pointing out familiar faces, remembering long-gone shops, imagining what might come next.

And the sounds — oh, the sounds. A fiddle found its voice near the café, joined by a guitar and a worn harmonica. The tune was rough around the edges, but it was enough to make toes tap and heads bob. The scent of barbecue floated in from a food stall at the square's edge, the promise of shared meals and full bellies.

Sophie wiped sweat from her brow and turned in a slow circle, taking it all in. The square — bruised, battered, but unbowed — was waking up. And this time, it wasn't waiting for outsiders or promises in polished brochures. This was Marigold's doing. Marigold's heartbeat.

She caught sight of Cal across the square, his shirt damp with effort, his hair mussed by the breeze. He was fixing a crooked planter box, but as if sensing her gaze, he looked up. And in that glance, brief and quiet, was everything: pride, possibility, and the fragile, growing bond between them that neither dared name.

Sophie and Cal in Sync

As the sun climbed higher, casting warm light over the square's rebirth, Sophie and Cal found themselves side by side more often than not. It wasn't planned — they just gravitated toward the same tasks, the same needs, the same quiet understanding that came without words. And in that easy rhythm, something rare began to bloom: partnership, unforced and unspoken.

Cal was lifting a heavy wooden signpost when Sophie appeared at his side, fingers slipping under the opposite end without waiting to be asked. Together, they carried it across the square, boots scuffing brick, shoulders brushing as they navigated the maze of ladders and volunteers. When they set it down, they both exhaled at the same moment — and laughed softly at the synchronicity.

"You're stronger than you look," Cal said, wiping sweat from his brow with the back of his hand. His smile was real, no longer edged with skepticism.

Sophie smirked, grabbing a hammer from the toolkit between them. "I've had to be."

Their banter wove through the day like thread through fabric. A shared glance when a teenager knocked over a paint can. A quick quip when Cal's crew discovered a nest of squirrels behind a loose shutter. Moments that would have been nothing days ago now felt like tiny stones building something solid beneath their feet.

At one point, they found themselves kneeling side by side, fixing the warped slats of a bench. Cal steadied the board as Sophie hammered, their hands brushing briefly. The contact was electric — not in the dramatic way of novels or films, but in the simple, honest shock of realizing how good closeness could feel.

For a heartbeat, Sophie hesitated, fingers resting against his. Cal didn't move, didn't speak. The world around them bustled with sound — voices, music, the creak of old wood being reborn — but between them was a pocket of stillness. A breath shared. A thought left unspoken.

When they finally straightened, Cal squinted at the square, the sun glinting off the newly cleaned windows, the bright splash of flowers in the planters. "Look at this," he said, voice low, almost reverent.

Sophie followed his gaze. The square wasn't finished. Not even close. But it was alive in a way it hadn't been in years. She swallowed hard, emotion thick in her throat. "It's what it could be," she said softly. "And maybe… what it used to be."

Cal glanced at her then — really looked — and for a moment, the rest of the world fell away. The laughter, the music, the clatter of tools — it all blurred at the edges. There was just this: two people, sweaty and tired, standing amid the mess and the beauty they'd helped create. The tension between them hummed, no longer sharp with doubt or frustration, but charged with something deeper. Something neither of them was ready to name. Not yet. But soon.

Sophie shifted first, tearing her gaze away to grab the next task. But as she passed him, her shoulder brushed his — a touch so small it could have been accidental. Could have been. Cal felt it, though. And he didn't step back.

They moved on, side by side, as the square continued to wake.

A Challenge Emerges

The square thrummed with energy — the kind that made Sophie's heart swell even as her muscles ached. She wiped her brow with the hem of her shirt, smudging a streak of dirt across her temple without noticing. Around her, people worked and laughed. A boy chased his little sister between freshly painted planters. Jeanine arranged weathered photographs in a window display. Cal hammered a new bracket onto a crooked railing, the steady rhythm of his work oddly soothing.

For a fleeting moment, Sophie let herself believe it. Believe in the hum of life returning, in the possibility that maybe — just maybe — this square could heal, and with it, all the fractures that had run through this town for so long.

But then she saw him.

At first, just a figure at the edge of the crowd — sharp suit, polished shoes out of place amid the scuffed boots and paint-flecked jeans. He stood beneath the shade of an old oak, arms crossed, tablet in hand. His eyes swept the scene with clinical detachment, as if cataloging not people, but assets.

The rival developer's representative — slick, practiced, and just detached enough to unsettle. Sophie knew who he was — the Atlanta firm's closer. Miles Whitcomb, or something equally smug. He'd been the name behind the renderings, the voice on the voicemail left for Jeanine, the hand behind the paper promises that now threatened to erase everything.

Her stomach knotted. The sunlight seemed harsher now, the laughter more fragile, as if one wrong move might crack the fragile joy that had taken root.

The man moved closer, weaving between groups with the smoothness of someone used to slipping into spaces uninvited. He smiled at volunteers, nodded at shopkeepers — all charm, no substance. Sophie's breath quickened when she saw him pause beside Councilman Walker, leaning in, voice low. Walker frowned, listening, glancing toward Sophie as if weighing invisible scales.

She stepped forward, heart pounding, but a hand on her elbow stopped her.

Cal.

"Let them watch," he said quietly. His hand was steady, warm. His voice anchored her. "We're not doing this for them."

Sophie looked up at him, saw the calm beneath the grit, the strength he drew from knowing what really mattered. The moment grounded her. She let out a slow breath, nodding. "You're right," she said, voice low.

But inside, fury and fear tangled. She hated that this man — this outsider with deep pockets and shallow promises — could sow doubt with a smirk and a whisper. Hated that after everything they'd built today, one polished presentation could still tempt some to forget what truly made Marigold home.

The developer's rep snapped a photo with his phone — the square, the people, the work in progress — and tucked his tablet under his arm like a man already counting the spoils. Sophie met his gaze across the distance, her expression steady, defiant. Let him see her. Let him see what resolve looked like.

Beside her, Cal's grip on the hammer tightened, but he said nothing more. His presence said enough. Together, they turned back to their work, shoulders brushing as they moved as one — choosing action over argument, hope over fear.

The rival's smirk faded as he watched them, perhaps realizing for the first time that this wasn't just about buildings or bids. This was about belonging. And that was harder to buy than bricks and mortar.

The Crowd Gathers

By midday, the square was no longer just a worksite — it was becoming a gathering place, the kind Sophie had dreamed of since she first set eyes on Marigold's heart again. The air smelled of cut grass, sun-warmed brick, and the sweet tang of barbecue from a smoker someone had wheeled out of a garage. The hum of conversation mingled with the soft strum of a guitar where a local musician had set up near the old bandstand, his case open, a few crumpled bills and coins resting inside.

Sophie straightened from where she'd been hauling a bucket of mulch to the planters and shaded her eyes. People drifted in from all corners of town — some out of curiosity, some drawn by the music and the scent of food, others by the undeniable energy that pulsed through the square like a second heartbeat.

She spotted Mr. Reed, the barber, leaning against his shop's doorway. His arms were crossed, but his gaze softened as he watched a group of teenagers paint the iron benches, their laughter ringing out every time someone smudged a shirt or got a stripe of green across a cheek.

Even the skeptics began to appear. Sophie caught sight of Mrs. Dawkins, cane in hand, peering over her spectacles at the fountain where Cal's crew had rigged a temporary water feature. The flow of water sparkled in the sunlight, drawing children like moths. They danced along the rim, splashing each other, their giggles filling spaces that had been silent too long.

Jeanine emerged from the bookstore, a battered camera slung around her neck. She snapped photos with quiet satisfaction — of the kids, the musicians, the banners strung between lampposts. Of hope made visible.

Cal appeared at Sophie's side, his shirt damp with sweat, a streak of sawdust on his jaw. He handed her a bottle of water, his hand brushing hers, and they shared a glance — wordless, but full of meaning.

"You see it?" he asked, voice low.

Sophie nodded, unable to speak for a moment. Her throat was thick with emotion. "I see it."

More came. Families pushing strollers. Retired couples, hand in hand. A group of high schoolers who'd once hung around the gas station now helping string more lights between the posts. The square filled with life — not perfect, not polished, but real.

Even those who didn't lift a hand stood and watched, drawn in despite themselves. The walls of doubt hadn't fallen, not entirely, but cracks showed — and in those cracks, sunlight streamed through.

For the first time since she'd returned to Marigold, Sophie felt the town begin to meet her halfway.

The Moment of Truth

The sun dipped low, casting the square in soft light, the kind that made the old brick glow like embers. The day's work left its mark everywhere Sophie looked: planters no longer choked by weeds, benches sporting fresh coats of paint, windows cleared of grime to reveal displays that spoke of the town's history and its hopes. The square wasn't finished — not by a long shot. But it was changed. And so was the crowd that now filled it.

Music drifted from the corner where the jazz trio had taken up their instruments, their notes mingling with the clink of iced tea glasses and the sizzle from the barbecue stall. Children's laughter rang out as they chased each other between tables. The tension of the morning, the uncertainty that had hung heavy for so long, seemed to ease, replaced by a cautious kind of pride.

Sophie wiped her hands on her jeans, her heart racing, not from exertion now, but from the weight of what came next. She hadn't planned a speech. But as she saw the faces turned toward her — expectant, tired, hopeful — she knew the moment called for words. Real ones.

Cal nudged her gently. "They're waiting for you," he murmured, his voice warm with something like admiration. His hand hovered at her back, as if steadying her without quite touching.

Sophie stepped forward, drawing a breath that tasted of summer and possibility. The crowd quieted as she raised her hands, not to command, but to invite.

"I didn't come back to Marigold for blueprints or permits," Sophie began, her voice cutting through the hush. "I came back because this place matters — not just the square, but everything around it. The people. The memories. The possibility of what we could become again, together.”

She glanced around, catching the eyes of people who’d doubted her, people who’d supported her, people who’d waited to see if she meant what she said.

“This isn’t about a plan on paper, or a grant, or any one person’s vision. It’s about what we can build together. What we *are* building. Today, you showed that. Every weed pulled, every brushstroke, every light strung — it mattered. You made this square come alive again. Not me. *You.*”

A ripple of applause, soft at first, then growing. Cal stepped beside her, looking out over the square with a quiet pride he didn’t try to hide anymore.

“This is just the beginning,” Sophie finished, her voice steady now, filled with resolve. “Let’s keep going. Let’s show everyone what Marigold can be when we rise together.”

The applause swelled — no roaring stadium cheer, but real, heartfelt clapping, joined by whistles, by whoops from the teenagers, by the unmistakable sound of community finding its voice.

And as the last of the sunlight faded, the string lights flickered on, casting the square in a soft, golden glow. Faces that had been wary now shone with cautious hope.

Sophie turned to Cal, breathless in the best way. “Thank you,” she said simply.

He shook his head. “No. *Thank you.*”

And for the first time, she believed they might really have a chance.

Cal and Sophie’s Emotional Shift

The crowd lingered as the sky deepened from gold to violet. Laughter mingled with the low hum of conversation, and for once, the square felt alive in the way Sophie had only dared imagine. The musicians packed up their instruments; children sprawled on the grass, too tired to run but unwilling to leave the magic of the moment. The scent of woodsmoke and barbecue still hung in the air, mingling with honeysuckle carried on the night breeze.

Sophie stood near the fountain, watching as neighbors who had once stood on opposite sides of every argument now shared stories over paper plates piled high with food. Volunteers she barely knew an hour ago now joked like old friends. It was the square as it was meant to be: not perfect, not finished — but *theirs*.

She sensed, more than saw, Cal come up beside her. His shirt clung to him with the dust and sweat of the day, sleeves rolled, hair damp at the temples. He smelled of cedar, smoke, and something unmistakably his. For a long moment, neither spoke. They just stood there, watching the town they loved — and maybe, finally, letting themselves feel it.

"You did good today," Cal said quietly, his voice rough from too little water and too many conversations. His gaze didn't leave the square, but Sophie felt the weight of his words settle warmly around her.

We. She almost said it aloud. *We did good.*

Instead, she risked a glance at him, and found he was already looking at her. And in that look was everything they hadn't said: the fights, the banter, the grudging respect that had grown into something steadier, deeper.

The glow of the string lights caught in his eyes, softening the lines of fatigue at their corners. He smiled — just barely — and without thinking, Sophie reached up, brushing a smudge of paint from his cheek. Her fingers lingered a beat too long, and when she realized it, her breath caught.

His hand rose, instinctively, as if to capture hers. But at the last second, he let it fall, shoving it into his pocket instead. The moment stretched between them, fragile and electric.

"Look at us," Cal murmured, shaking his head as if he couldn't quite believe it himself. "Square's cleaned up. People smiling. And I'm standing here thinking…" He trailed off, swallowing hard, as if afraid to finish.

Sophie's heart raced. "Thinking what?"

Cal hesitated, then gave a small, rueful laugh. "Thinking how easy it'd be to fall for you… and how much harder that would make everything else."

The words hung there, raw and honest. Sophie felt the square fall away — the chatter, the lights, the night itself — until it was just them, two tired souls standing on the edge of something neither had expected.

She didn't answer — not with words. Her fingers dropped beside his, a touch that spoke acceptance, hesitation, and something just beginning. The touch was light, but it was enough. Enough to say *me too*. Enough to promise *not yet, but soon*.

The tension between them wasn't sharp anymore. It was warm now, steady — like the glow of the lights strung over their heads, like the town itself: battered, but shining all the same.

Someone called Cal's name from across the square — his crew packing up. The spell broke, gently, like waking from a dream.

He stepped back, but not far. His voice was low, meant only for her. "I'll see you tomorrow, Sophie."

And she, for once, didn't feel the need to fill the silence. She just nodded, watching as he walked away, his silhouette framed by the lights and the life they'd fought for all day.

When he disappeared into the crowd, Sophie exhaled, slow and deep. Her chest ached in the best way — full of hope, and fear, and the sweet, terrifying possibility of something real.

And still, the square glowed on — not finished, but undeniably alive with promise.

Chapter 14

Setbacks and Sparks

Morning came with the soft light of dawn slipping through thin curtains, painting the room in muted gold. Sophie stirred, sore in places she didn't know could ache — her hands tender from hauling lumber, shoulders tight from hours of work, legs heavy from climbing ladders and crossing the square a dozen times over. But beneath the exhaustion, a quiet satisfaction hummed. *Yesterday mattered.* For the first time in months — maybe years — she felt it in her bones: they'd done something real.

She sat up slowly, listening to the square wake below. The sound of a broom sweeping a sidewalk, the clatter of a shop shutter being raised, birdsong threading through it all. She allowed herself a small, private smile. *Maybe… maybe this is the turning point.*

Her phone buzzed on the nightstand, shattering the moment's peace. She reached for it, expecting a thank-you message, maybe a photo someone had taken during Square Revival Day.

Instead, her breath hitched as she read the subject line of the email blinking on the screen:

Formal Proposal Submitted — Riverstone Development Marigold Redevelopment Plan

Her heart sank.

She clicked through, fingers trembling slightly. The body of the email was terse — a copy of the submission letter sent to the council,

CC'd to key stakeholders. Attached were glossy renderings: sleek buildings, wide boulevards, promises of fast-tracked permits, job creation numbers, tax revenue projections that would make any struggling town council pause.

Sophie's chest tightened. She scrolled through the images, the corporate speak, the bullet points. Cold, efficient. Everything she wasn't. Everything that might undo all they'd fought for yesterday.

A knock at the door made her jump. She hastily shut her laptop and crossed to open it, composing her face. When she swung the door wide, Cal stood there, holding two cups of coffee. His shirt was rumpled; his eyes, like hers, were shadowed by too little sleep.

"Thought you could use this," he said, offering a cup.

She took it, grateful for the warmth in her hands. "You have good timing."

His brow furrowed. "What happened?"

She stepped back to let him in, closing the door gently behind them. The room smelled of sawdust clinging to his clothes, mingling with the sharp scent of coffee. For a heartbeat, she wished they could just stay in this small, suspended moment — no square, no council, no rival proposals. Just two people, tired and trying.

Instead, she opened the laptop again, turning it so he could see. "The rival developer filed. It's official now. And they're trying to push the council before our thirty days are even up."

Cal scanned the screen, jaw tightening. He muttered something under his breath she couldn't quite catch, but the tone needed no translation.

The silence that followed was heavy, the kind that comes when hope starts to slip through your fingers. Finally, he spoke. "Well. That didn't take them long."

Sophie sank onto the sofa, coffee balanced on her knee. "No. It didn't."

He paced, restless, running a hand through his hair. "They're throwing everything at us. Money. Promises. All the things this town's been told to want for years."

She watched him, exhaustion giving way to quiet dread. "And what if the town wants it, Cal? What if they choose the easy answer?"

He stopped pacing, met her gaze. And in that moment, she saw the weight he carried — the weight they both carried now. "Then we remind them why this place matters. Why it's worth fighting for."

His words steadied her, a little. But beneath them, the shadow of the proposal loomed. The day that had begun with the promise of rebuilding now bristled with the threat of being erased. The thirty-day cushion they'd fought for? Gone in a flash. The temporary fix had bought them time — but not enough.

Cal sat beside her, their shoulders brushing. No speeches. No plans yet. Just coffee cooling between them, and the square outside holding its breath for what would come next.

Tension Rises

The square that had felt so alive yesterday now seemed brittle — as if one hard wind might shatter it. As if one hard wind might shatter what they'd built. Cal and Sophie walked side by side down Main Street, steaming coffee in hand, the warmth doing little to cut the chill that had settled between them.

Shopkeepers lifted blinds, swept stoops. A few nodded their way, but Sophie could sense the change — eyes that yesterday had glowed with cautious hope now darted away, uncertain, calculating.

"They're already talking, aren't they?" Sophie murmured.

Cal didn't answer at first. He took a sip of his coffee, watching as old Mr. Reed, the barber, stepped out of his shop and studied the square like a man measuring loss.

"Yeah," Cal said finally. "They're talking. You can't blame 'em. A town like this? We don't get offers like that every day. And people start to wonder — if what we're building is hope, or just a delay. That other plan... it looks safe. Polished. Finished. Ours still has dirt under its nails."

The words weren't meant to hurt, but they did. Sophie felt them lodge in her chest like splinters. *Was that what he thought, too?*

She stopped walking, turning to face him fully. The square stretched behind him, sunlight catching on the fountain's worn edges, the newly scrubbed benches, the banners still flapping from Square Revival Day. All of it suddenly fragile.

"Is that what you think?" she asked, quieter than she meant.

Cal hesitated, torn between honesty and kindness. "I think—" He exhaled hard, raking a hand through his hair. "I think I want to believe what we're doing is enough. But I'm scared too, Sophie. I'm scared we'll lose everything anyway. And I don't know if I can watch that happen."

There it was. The crack in his armor she'd always sensed but never seen so clearly. And it rattled her — because it echoed the crack in her own.

"You can't have it both ways," she said, voice tight. "You want change, but you're afraid of it. You want me to help fix this place, but the second it gets hard, you pull back."

Cal's eyes flashed. "That's not fair."

"Isn't it?" she shot back. The tension that had been simmering between them, the unspoken worries, the weight of the town's future — it all came boiling to the surface.

"I'm not afraid of change," Cal said, voice low, steady. "I'm afraid of losing what little we have left. I'm afraid of waking up one morning and seeing this town turned into something I don't recognize, because I trusted the wrong plan. The wrong person." His gaze didn't waver, but the softness beneath the frustration was undeniable. "Don't ask me not to care, Sophie. This place — it's my whole damn life."

Sophie's anger ebbed, leaving only the ache beneath. "And you think I don't care?" Her voice broke at the edges. "You think I'm here risking everything because I don't care?"

The space between them was taut, charged. They stood at the center of the square, the early morning bustle of the town forgotten — their world narrowed to this moment, two people caught between fear and faith, between what they wanted and what they were terrified to hope for.

Cal's shoulders sagged, some of the fire in him cooling. "No. I know you care. That's the hardest part."

For a beat, neither of them spoke. Around them, Marigold stirred: the creak of a shop sign in the breeze, the low hum of a truck passing by, the chatter of two teenagers cutting across the square. Life went on, indifferent to the storm brewing inside them.

Finally, Sophie drew a breath, trying to steady herself. "We can't do this like enemies, Cal. If we don't stand together, that developer wins without lifting a finger."

Cal nodded slowly, the fight in him tempered by something quieter — resolve. "Then we stand together."

It wasn't a truce born of perfect agreement. It was messier than that — two people tangled in doubt, clinging to the one thing they had left: each other.

Council Divided

By mid-morning, the town council chamber felt more like a tinderbox than a meeting room. Sunlight slanted through the tall windows, catching in dust motes that swirled like anxious thoughts. Sophie sat near the front, back straight, hands folded tightly in her lap — the picture of composure on the outside, a riot of worry on the inside.

The council members trickled in: Hester Boyd, calm but visibly worn; Tom Abernathy, his jaw clenched like he'd already made up his mind; Marsha Lang, adjusting her glasses as she shuffled through the rival developer's glossy packet. Around them, the usual scattering of residents filled the rows of creaky chairs — not as many as at the revival day, but enough to make the room hum with tension.

Jeanine caught Sophie's eye from the back row, giving the faintest nod — the kind that said *steady now*. Sophie breathed it in like oxygen.

Councilwoman Boyd called the meeting to order, her gavel falling with a dull thud that felt more like punctuation to an argument than the start of one.

"We're here today to discuss the formal proposal submitted by Riverstone Development," Hester began, voice carefully neutral. "And to hear preliminary reactions from the community. No vote will be taken today."

But Sophie saw the way Marsha and Tom leaned toward each other, whispering behind raised hands. She saw the way a few shop owners — ones who'd smiled at her just days ago — avoided her gaze now, their faces shuttered with uncertainty.

The developer's representative stood to speak — Miles Whitcomb, the same man Sophie had spotted beneath the oak during Square Revival Day, all sharp suit and smooth edges. His smile was just as practiced now, his voice just as polished as he outlined Riverstone's pitch: expedited timelines, injections of capital, modern infrastructure, "job creation opportunities" he didn't bother to define. The words came slick and fast, a flood of promises gilded in numbers and jargon.

Some in the room leaned in, drawn to the glitter. Sophie felt the shift in the air, the weight of hope and fear tangled together. It was a powerful lure — quick money, quick fixes. Exactly what desperate towns were primed to grasp for.

When the man finished, murmurs rippled through the room. Tom Abernathy cleared his throat, clearly impressed. Marsha tapped her pen thoughtfully against her notepad.

It was Jeanine who stood next. She didn't move to the podium — she didn't need to. Her voice, clear and steady, carried without it.

"I'm not much for numbers," she said, tone warm but firm. "I leave those to smarter folk. But I've lived here long enough to know you can't put a price on what makes Marigold ours. You can't slap a new coat of paint on a thing and call it saved. What we've started here — what Sophie's started — isn't easy, isn't fast. But it's ours. This square, these streets — they carry our story. And that matters."

A hush followed, the kind that hangs when truth has been spoken aloud.

Sophie's throat tightened. She hadn't expected Jeanine to speak. The gratitude welled up, sharp and sudden.

But the division was clear. Some in the crowd nodded, their faces softening with remembered loyalty to the town they loved. Others frowned, caught between the comfort of familiar streets and the siren call of new prosperity.

Councilwoman Boyd glanced around, as if weighing the room. "We appreciate all perspectives," she said, measured. "This council will give both proposals fair consideration. We owe that to the community."

Sophie wanted to speak, to rise and counter the developer's promises point by point. But something stopped her — the sense that today was for listening, for seeing where the true lines had been drawn. She'd have her chance. But first, she had to understand what she was up against.

The meeting adjourned with no decisions, just the murmur of voices as people filed out — some hopeful, some hesitant, some already caught in the rival plan's glittering net.

Sophie lingered at the front of the chamber, heart heavy, as Jeanine came to stand beside her.

"They heard you," Sophie whispered. "They heard what you meant."

Jeanine's smile was small, but sure. "Maybe. But hearing's not the same as believing. You know that, don't you?"

Sophie nodded, watching as Cal slipped out the back, his face unreadable.

The lines were drawn. The next move was hers.

Sophie and Cal, Alone Again

The sun was low, casting the square in long shadows that seemed to stretch out the day's troubles. Sophie sat on the fountain's edge, shoulders slumped, her hands resting limply in her lap. The hum of insects filled the silence, the town's usual evening chatter subdued, as if Marigold itself was holding its breath.

The fountain's cracked basin caught the fading light, its dry surface streaked with the ghost of water that once ran clear. Sophie stared at it, seeing not the stone, but the weight of promises she'd made — to her mother, to herself, to this town — and wondering if they were slipping through her fingers like sand.

The sound of boots on brick made her lift her head. Cal approached slowly, no longer the man who challenged her at meetings or sparred with her over plans. His face was soft in the dusk, worry etched around his eyes, but not just for the town — for her.

"Thought I might find you here," he said quietly, hands shoved deep in his pockets.

Sophie didn't look at him at first. She kept her gaze on the fountain, swallowing hard against the tightness in her throat. "It felt right to be here. Or maybe I didn't know where else to go."

Cal settled beside her, leaving just enough space for the night air between them. For a moment they sat in silence, listening to the square's quiet heartbeat.

"You didn't have to speak for people to feel it. You've already said enough by what you've done."

Sophie laughed softly, the sound bitter at the edges. "Did I? Because right now it feels like I'm watching it all slip away. Like I'm failing her — my mother. Failing everyone."

Her voice cracked, and she hated that it did.

Cal turned, his gaze steady. "You're not failing anyone. You're fighting for something real. That's more than most people do."

She shook her head. "What if fighting isn't enough? What if I'm just... forcing something this town doesn't even want anymore?"

Cal was quiet for a long beat. When he spoke, his voice was lower, almost a confession. "After Lena died, I spent a lot of nights sitting where you are — trying to keep things steady for Emma. Staring at this fountain, at this square. Wondering how I was supposed to hold it all together. The business. The kid. Myself." He gave a short, humorless laugh. "Most days, I still don't know."

Sophie's heart squeezed. The Cal she saw now wasn't the gruff defender of old brick and stubborn traditions. He was a man laid bare by grief, by responsibility, by the same weight she carried.

"I thought if I could just keep things the same — the square, the shop, our routines — maybe Emma wouldn't feel how broken things were," he went on. "Maybe I wouldn't."

Sophie turned then, really seeing him. The weariness. The honesty. The hope he tried so hard to keep hidden. She felt the distance between them shrink, not in inches, but in understanding.

"I get it," she said softly. "I thought if I came back here and fixed this place, maybe I'd fix what I left behind. Maybe I'd stop feeling like I let her down."

Their eyes met, the square falling away until there was only this — two people bound by loss, by longing, by the terrifying possibility of hope.

The air between them changed, charged now, as if the night itself held its breath. Cal's hand twitched, as if he meant to reach for hers. Sophie leaned in, drawn by something bigger than either of them — the need for comfort, for connection, for something solid in a world that felt like it could crumble at any moment.

And then — just as his fingers brushed hers, just as the space between them vanished — a sound broke the spell. A door creaked open across the square, voices echoed faintly from the café's back porch. Reality returned like a cold breeze.

They pulled back, the moment slipping through their hands, too heavy with everything that hadn't been said.

Cal exhaled, slow and shaky. "Sophie…"

She smiled, small and sad. "I know."

And they sat there, the weight of the night pressing close, neither ready to leave, neither quite able to cross that last inch — not yet.

The Developer Makes a Move

Night fell over Marigold like a slow exhale, the kind that left the air thick and restless. Sophie finally left the fountain when the square was nearly empty, save for the hum of a streetlamp and the rustle of leaves in the breeze. She made her way back home, weary to her core. The conversation with Cal lingered — warm, painful, unfinished — like the ghost of a song half-remembered.

But peace would not last the night.

Before dawn, the town began to stir for all the wrong reasons.

As she dressed, she paused at the window, scanning the square. Something was off. On nearly every doorstep, porch swing, and shop stoop, the morning light caught the gleam of glossy paper — thick envelopes, tri-fold brochures, branded folders stamped with a logo she now recognized instantly: Riverstone Development.

Her heart sank.

By the time she reached her porch, she didn't need to open the packet to know what was inside. But she did.

The same proposal — only slicker. Same soulless vision. Same fountain replaced by a steel sculpture. Same sterile plazas, copy-paste storefronts, and vague promises of jobs and tax revenue. But now it came dressed in community language, neighborly fonts, and curated photos of towns they'd "revitalized."

This time, it wasn't aimed at the council. It was aimed at hearts and minds — at everyone.

From across the square, she saw curtains twitch. Mr. Abernathy — one of the council's most reluctant holdouts — stepped onto his porch, packet in hand, brow furrowed as he read. Down the block, Mrs. Dawkins clutched hers like a lifeline, nodding as she scanned the bold print. The message was working. Not with truth — but with polish.

The café door creaked open. Jeanine stepped out, a packet tucked under her arm. Their eyes met. No words. Just a small, grim nod.

They both knew: Riverstone had made its move — and it was a smart one. Strategic. Psychological. Designed not to persuade, but to erode.

Sophie's fingers curled tighter around the packet, as if she could crush its influence by force of will alone. The square — so full of light just days ago — now looked exposed. Vulnerable. Like something that could be lost before the fight truly began.

She turned back toward her house, toward the room where her blueprints waited. But on the porch steps, she paused. Looked back. The rival's vision was slicker. Louder. Funded by deeper pockets. But it didn't have what she had.

It didn't have *them.*

It didn't have *heart.*

Resolve settled beneath her ribs like bedrock, even as anxiety whispered along the edges.

At her desk, she dropped the packet beside her notes and stared out the window as the town stirred — each person waking to a choice they hadn't expected to face so soon.

The square was still beautiful in the morning sun.

Still worth fighting for.

Her mother's voice echoed inside her, not a memory this time — but a calling.

Even if the fight had just gotten harder, and far more personal.

She reached for her pencil.

And started drafting.

Chapter 15

Lines Drawn

By midmorning, Marigold no longer felt like the same town Sophie had come to love — or fight for. The square, usually a place of easy smiles and neighborly nods, now buzzed with tension thick enough to taste. Sophie stood near the fountain, watching as people moved through the space with new caution. Conversations that once happened out in the open were now reduced to hushed murmurs in tight circles. Eyes darted away when she passed, or worse — held her gaze too long, filled with a blend of hope, worry, and doubt she couldn't quite read.

The glossy packets from the rival developer had done their work. This wasn't just a pitch — it was a quiet invasion.

Not handed out at a meeting, not pinned to a bulletin board. It had arrived at every doorstep like a foregone conclusion, like the town had already agreed without her.

That was what stung the most.

The same proposal — only slicker. Same soulless vision. Same fountain replaced by a sculpture of cold steel. Same sterile plazas and vague promises of jobs and tax revenue. But now it came dressed in community language, with neighborly fonts, curated snapshots of "revitalized" towns, and pull quotes that felt eerily tailored.

She saw the packets clutched under arms, folded into handbags, half-hidden beneath café menus. Their bright promises had seeped into the town's cracks, not as policy, but as persuasion.

From across the square, curtains twitched. Mr. Abernathy stepped out with his packet, brow furrowed. Down the block, Mrs. Dawkins clutched hers like gospel. Even the café had one, resting beside the register like a free sample.

This wasn't lobbying. It was seduction.

And as Sophie stood at the edge of the square — the same square they had just begun to reclaim — she felt, for the first time, not just the weight of a rival's offer… but the cold edge of a town beginning to turn.

She moved from shop to shop, stopping at the bakery where Mrs. Tolliver greeted her with a warm, if wary, smile.

"You holding up, dear?" the woman asked, sliding a small paper bag across the counter — a sticky bun Sophie hadn't ordered.

"Trying," Sophie admitted, accepting the quiet kindness.

But even here, the mood was different. A group at the window table lowered their voices as she passed, their conversation shifting from casual to cautious.

On Main Street, she paused outside the barbershop. Inside, Cal's friend, Art, was sweeping the floor. When he noticed her, he hesitated — then gave a small wave that didn't quite reach his eyes. Sophie stepped inside.

"Just checking in," she said lightly. "Seeing how folks are feeling."

Art set his broom aside. "Split down the middle, if you want the truth. Some folks… they're dazzled by the promises. Big money talks, you know that." He looked at her, softened by guilt. "But others — we see what you're trying to do. We just don't know if it's enough."

That's what stung the most — not anger or rejection, but doubt. Quiet, creeping doubt that could hollow out everything she'd worked for.

As Sophie stepped back into the square, the place felt like a battleground dressed in small-town charm. The same bunting from Square Revival Day still fluttered between lamp posts, but now it seemed like a memory of optimism slipping away.

She spotted Hester Boyd on the courthouse steps, speaking in low tones with two other council members. They glanced in Sophie's direction. Hester's expression was unreadable — somewhere between sympathy and calculation. Sophie forced a smile, nodded, and kept walking.

Her steps slowed as she approached the café. The rival's renderings were displayed in the window, tacked up next to a flyer for the town's spring festival. Sophie's heart clenched at the sight — modern facades, sleek plazas, a Marigold unrecognizable.

Inside, Jeanine watched from a corner table, her face a mask of quiet determination. Their eyes met, and Jeanine lifted her coffee cup in a silent toast of solidarity. The gesture was small, but it steadied Sophie's resolve.

Still, as she continued down the street, Sophie couldn't deny the truth: the town was divided. The promises of quick prosperity had taken root in fertile soil — fear, exhaustion, the longing for an easier path. And Sophie knew that whatever came next, she'd be fighting not just a developer, but the cracks in the town's heart itself.

Sophie Strategizes

The soft chime of the bookstore's doorbell broke the heavy stillness of the evening. Sophie stepped inside, brushing a stray hair from her face, shoulders tight with fatigue. The scent of old paper and tea leaves calmed her — or tried to. Tonight, the cozy shop felt less like a refuge, more like a war room.

Jeanine was waiting. She had already cleared the big oak table in the back, save for a pot of tea, a half-eaten biscuit, and a stack of yellowed town maps. The dim light from the desk lamp cast long shadows across the walls lined with history.

"Come on," Jeanine said, no greeting needed. "Let's get to work."

A few others trickled in — Naomi Tolliver from the bakery, Sam from the garage, two teens Sophie had seen helping on Square Revival

Day. No more than a half dozen souls, but their presence mattered. It meant she wasn't fighting alone.

Sophie spread out her papers — plans, budgets, mock-ups — the bones of her vision laid bare. The air hummed with quiet intensity.

"We need to move fast," Sophie began, her voice low but firm. "The developer's promises are everywhere. If we let them control the story, we lose before we start."

Jeanine leaned forward. "What's your plan?"

"First, a petition — and it needs to move fast. We'll set up at the café, the store, maybe even the school if they'll allow it. Online too. Social media can work for us — not just them."

Sam grunted. "Folks will sign. But will they show up?"

Sophie didn't flinch. "We give them a reason. A town hall, open to everyone. We make our case in the open — not just to the council, but to each other. Remind people what's at stake, what we can build together."

Naomi nodded, eyes sharp. "You'll need more than speeches."

"I know." Sophie hesitated, then laid out another sheet — a rough action timeline. "We showcase what we've already done. The Square Revival Day — photos, stories. We highlight the businesses that have pledged support, the local jobs we're creating. We make it real. And we need voices — not just mine. Cal's. Yours. People who are trusted."

A hush fell. The group knew the stakes. Knew the odds.

Jeanine broke it. "It's a good plan. A hard one. But good. You've got allies, Sophie. Maybe not enough yet, but more than you had yesterday." She poured tea into Sophie's cup, hands steady. "Now let's map it out."

They worked deep into the night. Maps unrolled, names brainstormed, schedules drafted. Sophie's heart thudded in time with the scratch of pens and the creak of the shop's old floorboards. For every idea, she worried it wouldn't be enough. For every tactic, she feared the developer's money would drown them out.

But as midnight neared and the group disbanded, she felt it — the first flicker of hope she'd felt all day. They had a plan. They had each other.

As she stepped out into the night, the square lay silent under a wash of stars. The town was still divided. The battle lines had been drawn. But Sophie wasn't retreating. Not now. Not ever.

Cal's Dilemma

The workshop smelled of cedar and motor oil, the scent of honest labor. Cal stood at the workbench, hands braced on either side of a splintered board, as if he could steady himself by sheer force of will. His crew sat scattered across the room — some perched on toolboxes, others leaning against saw horses, their faces lined with fatigue, worry, and unspoken questions.

"You hear about the developer's offer?" Cal asked, though he already knew the answer.

Murmurs of assent. One of the older men, Pete, shifted uncomfortably. "Cal, we gotta face it. Folks are scared. The money they're promising… it'd fix a lot of things around here. Fast."

Cal clenched his jaw, staring at the grooves etched deep into the wood beneath his palms. Fast. Easy. Those words always came with a price. And Marigold had paid it before — with shuttered shops, with families who left and never came back, with dreams crumbled like old brick.

"I know," he said finally. His voice was quiet, but carried. "But fast money doesn't rebuild trust. It doesn't give us back what we lost."

Silence followed, heavy as the humid night air pressing through the open door.

One of the younger guys, Tommy, spoke up — hesitant, but honest. "What if they're right, Cal? What if this is the only shot we get?"

Cal didn't answer right away. He looked out into the darkened street beyond the workshop, where the square sat in shadow. He thought of the fountain, dry and broken. The empty storefronts. The weight of responsibility — not just for the work, but for what came after.

And he thought of Sophie.

The stubborn set of her shoulders as she faced down doubters. The light in her eyes when she spoke of the town's potential. The way she'd made him believe — almost — that rebuilding wasn't just possible, but worth it.

"I can't stop anyone from chasing what looks easy," Cal said at last, turning back to his crew. "But I'm not doing this for easy. I'm doing it for what's right. And I hope to hell you'll stand with me."

They nodded, some reluctantly, some with conviction. The bond of shared labor, tested and true.

Later, at home, the quiet was deafening. Cal sat at the edge of Emma's bed, watching as she fought sleep, her small face relaxed in the soft glow of the nightlight.

"Daddy?" Her voice was drowsy, but clear.

"Yeah, baby."

"Is Miss Sophie gonna fix the fountain?"

The question hit him harder than he expected. Simple. Pure. And packed with the weight of everything he was fighting for.

"I think she will," he said softly. "If we let her."

Emma's eyes drifted closed, her trust complete, her world still small enough that hope seemed easy. Cal sat there a long time after, listening to her even breathing, the quiet ticking of the old clock in the hall, the distant hum of the night.

And he knew: whatever choice the town made, whatever storm came next — he was in it. For Emma. For the square. For Sophie. For the promise they all deserved.

For all of it.

A Chance Encounter

The night settled over Marigold like a quilt stitched from shadow and silence. Main Street was deserted now, the shop windows dark, the square empty but for the soft glow of a single lamplight flickering near the fountain. Sophie walked alone, arms crossed against the cool night breeze, head bowed beneath the weight of the day.

Her boots echoed on the cracked pavement, each step slow, reluctant. She wasn't ready to return home — not yet. The square felt different tonight. Not hostile, but wary. As if the town itself was holding its breath, waiting to see which way the wind would blow.

A soft sound — the creak of a door — made her glance up. Cal emerged from the workshop across the street, locking up for the night. For a moment, he didn't see her. His shoulders were hunched with exhaustion, his stride heavy. But then his gaze lifted, and their eyes met across the quiet street.

Neither spoke at first. The distance between them felt both impossibly wide and achingly small.

Cal crossed toward her, his boots scuffing against the curb. The lamplight caught the lines of his face, the weariness in his eyes, the tension still coiled in his frame.

"You couldn't sleep either?" he asked, voice low.

Sophie shook her head. "Didn't try."

They stood together, the fountain between them, dry and silent — a reminder of everything unfinished.

For a long moment, neither spoke. The weight of the day — the whispered doubts, the council's looming decision, the fear of failure — hung between them like fog.

Finally, Sophie broke the silence. "I thought today was hard," she said, her voice soft but steady. "But tomorrow's going to be worse, isn't it?"

Cal's lips quirked in a humorless smile. "Most likely."

Their eyes met again, and something shifted. The air between them felt charged — not with argument or frustration, but with understanding. The kind that comes only when two people have fought on the same side, even if they didn't always agree on how.

"I'm tired of fighting," Sophie admitted, her voice barely above a whisper. "But I don't know how to stop."

"You don't stop," Cal said quietly. "You just… rest where you can. And then you keep going."

She looked at him then — really looked. At the man who had challenged her at every turn, who had questioned her motives and tested her resolve. And yet, here he was. At her side. When it mattered.

Their hands brushed as they both leaned on the fountain's edge, and neither pulled away. The warmth of that brief contact sent a jolt through Sophie's chest — unexpected and undeniable. She saw the flicker in Cal's eyes, felt the pull between them like a thread drawn taut.

For a heartbeat, the world narrowed to just this: the glow of the lamplight, the quiet night, the closeness of him.

But then Cal straightened, breaking the spell. His voice was rough with something unsaid. "We'll get through this, Sophie. One way or another."

Sophie nodded, swallowing the ache in her throat. "Yeah. We will."

They stood in silence a moment longer, the distance between them closing in ways that had nothing to do with space.

And then, without another word, they parted — each walking back toward their own worries, their own sleepless nights. But with the promise, unspoken but felt, that they wouldn't be facing them alone.

The Challenge Issued

Morning arrived in Marigold beneath a bruised sky, clouds heavy with the threat of rain — or perhaps it was only the mood of the town that made the day feel so gray. By the time Sophie stepped onto Main Street, the news had already spread.

The notice was nailed to the bulletin board outside town hall, the paper crisp, the lettering bold:

EMERGENCY TOWN MEETING — ALL RESIDENTS

INVITED

Agenda: Final presentations on the future of the town square. Formal proposals by competing parties to be heard. Council vote to follow.

The time: two days from now.

The location: the old town hall where generations had gathered to debate, to argue, to choose.

Sophie stood before the notice, heart hammering. The words blurred at the edges as the weight of what lay ahead settled over her like a stone. This was it. The final chance to convince the town, to save the square — and, in some ways, to save herself.

The air around her buzzed with tension as townsfolk paused to read the notice, murmuring to one another in hushed tones. Some faces were hopeful; others, wary. A few avoided her gaze altogether.

Behind her, the sound of steady footsteps made her turn. Cal approached, hands shoved in his jacket pockets, jaw tight with unspoken thoughts.

Their eyes met, and in that glance, so much passed between them — fear, resolve, weariness, and something else, too: the knowledge that whatever came next, they were in it together.

He stopped beside her, studied the notice for a long moment, then exhaled slowly. "Well," he said, his voice low, "looks like the battle lines are drawn."

Sophie nodded, swallowing the dryness in her throat. "I guess they are."

A beat of silence. The town square stretched out before them, the heart of Marigold caught between past and future, hope and surrender.

Cal glanced at her, his tone softening. "We'll face it. One step at a time."

Sophie looked out over the square, imagining it as it could be — and as it might be lost. And in that moment, with Cal beside her, she felt the first spark of steel beneath the fear.

"Together?" she asked, the question as much about the fight as about them.

Cal didn't hesitate. "Together."

The storm was coming — but this time, Sophie knew she wouldn't be facing it alone.

Chapter 16

The Town Meeting

The night air was thick, the kind that clung to skin and seemed to carry every whisper, every worry. From blocks away, Sophie could see the glow of the town hall — brighter than she could remember. Its windows shone like beacons, lighting the worn clapboard siding, throwing long, skewed shadows of people gathered on the lawn. The building that so often stood empty now pulsed with purpose — and fear.

She approached slowly, heart thudding, breath shallow. It felt less like walking toward a meeting and more like stepping onto a stage — or a battlefield. The square she'd come to love, with all its cracks and quirks, had funneled its hopes and divisions into this one night.

The steps overflowed with residents. People she'd shared coffee with, nodded to on morning walks, waved to as they swept their porches — now clustered in tight knots, voices low, faces tense. She caught snippets as she passed:

"...this might be our only chance..."

"...what about the soul of the town? You can't rebuild that with concrete and glass..."

"...money's money, and we sure as hell need it..."

The words bit at her resolve. Each one a reminder of what she was up against — not just a developer with deep pockets, but the exhaustion, the hunger for relief that made even bad deals sound sweet.

Inside, the hall groaned beneath the weight of its occupants. Every bench, every inch of floor was claimed — men, women, children perched on laps, babies fussing against the tension that thickened the air. The smell of damp wool, wood polish, and too many bodies filled her nose.

Sophie slipped in through the side door, clutching her folder of notes and mockups so tightly her knuckles went white. She chose a seat near the front, spreading her papers on the scarred table before her — diagrams she'd drawn a hundred times, now blurring at the edges from wear and worry.

She tried to still her hands. They trembled despite herself. She closed her eyes for a moment, reaching for the memory of her mother's voice — calm, certain, telling her as a child that home was worth fighting for, no matter the odds.

When she opened them again, she caught sight of Cal.

He'd entered through the main doors, taller than most in the crowd, his face set and unreadable. He moved slowly through the room, offering nods, a clasp on a shoulder here, a quiet word there — gestures that spoke volumes where words would have felt hollow. His gaze swept the room and landed on Sophie, just for a beat. A flicker of something — solidarity, maybe, or shared dread — passed between them. Then he turned, settling near the back, arms folded, as if bracing for impact.

The gavel came down, sharp and final.

"The special session of the Marigold Town Council is now in order," Hester Boyd said, her voice carrying above the murmur like the snap of a flag in the wind. "Let's conduct ourselves with respect. We'll hear the proposals in turn. Remember — this isn't just about buildings. This is about Marigold's future."

The murmurs quieted. The hall seemed to hold its breath.

The Developer's Pitch

They had pitched before — sleek slides, smooth talk, and numbers stacked like scaffolding. But that had been at a council meeting, aimed at officials behind a dais, buffered by formalities. This was something else. This time, it wasn't just about strategy. It was spectacle. Public theater. A bid not for approval, but for allegiance. The developers had adapted — and now, they weren't trying to win over a few votes. They were trying to win the town.

The rival team rose as one — suits crisp, shoes polished to mirrors, their confidence filling the room before they spoke a word. The lead presenter — a man with silver hair, skin smooth as porcelain, and a voice like velvet — strode to the front. His smile was easy, practiced, as if he'd won this fight a hundred times before.

"Good evening, friends," he began, letting the word settle, as if he truly believed it. "We're here because, like you, we see the potential in this wonderful town."

He gestured, and with a flick of his wrist, the projector cast bright, pristine images across the faded beadboard wall. The contrast was stark — glossy, modern visions layered over the scars of history.

A new Marigold square gleamed on the screen: sleek glass-fronted shops, wide walkways lined with uniform planters, a fountain redesigned into something abstract and coldly beautiful. Rooftop patios glittered under imagined sunsets. Parking decks blended seamlessly into the landscape. Everything clean. Efficient. Unrecognizable.

He spoke of progress. Of prosperity. Of jobs created and tax bases expanded. He painted a picture of a town reborn — not in the image of what it had been, but in what outsiders might expect: polished, marketable, safe. His words slid through the room like oil over water: "Economic growth," "infrastructure investment," "future-proofing your community."

Sophie's gut twisted. She watched faces — saw how the numbers dazzled, how the promises soothed the weary and the worried. She saw Mr. Abernathy nodding, his usual scowl smoothed by dreams of solvency. She saw Mrs. Dawkins clutching her husband's hand, hope warring with doubt in her eyes.

But she also saw the unease. The flickers of uncertainty. Jeanine, seated near the center aisle, sat stiff and still — arms crossed, mouth tight, eyes narrowed like someone reading between the lines. The way Cal's jaw flexed, his fists clenched behind crossed arms as he stared at the renderings, seeing — Sophie knew — not salvation, but erasure.

The presenter's voice softened as he closed: "We're not here to erase Marigold. We're here to polish its potential and help it shine brighter than ever before. Let us help you build a future worthy of this town's promise."

The room exhaled in scattered applause — polite, uneven. Some clapped because they were moved. Others because they felt they should. And some didn't clap at all.

Sophie drew a breath so deep it hurt. It was her turn.

Sophie's Stand

The hall settled into uneasy quiet as the rival team stepped back, their glossy proposal lingering on the screen like a ghost of what could be — or what might be lost.

Sophie rose slowly, feeling every eye in the room shift to her. The weight of expectation, doubt, hope, and weariness pressed against her chest, making it hard to draw breath. Her hands brushed the edge of the table — not for the notes she'd prepared, but for grounding. Steady. Steady.

She looked at the papers she'd so carefully organized — bullet points, cost analyses, restoration timelines — and she saw them for what they were in this moment: inadequate. Numbers couldn't answer what hung in the air tonight. Spreadsheets wouldn't save the square.

So she set the papers aside.

She stepped forward, feeling the creak of the old floorboards beneath her boots, and let her gaze travel over the faces before her: the faces of Marigold. People who'd smiled at her on the street, who'd doubted her in meetings, who'd trusted her with a tentative nod or turned away in frustration. People she'd come to care about. People she didn't want to fail.

"My mother used to tell me," Sophie began, her voice quiet at first, but clear, "that the heart of a town isn't its buildings. It's the space between them — the spaces where we come together. The square. The park bench where she sat with me on summer nights. The café table where my parents planned our future. The fountain where we made wishes."

She paused, glancing at that shimmering rendering still glowing behind her — a version of Marigold that might as well have been another planet.

"This proposal," she said, gesturing toward the screen, "it's beautiful. It promises so much. Jobs. Growth. A quick fix for all the things that have gone wrong. And I won't stand here and tell you jobs and growth aren't important. They are. We need them."

Her eyes softened, her voice steady now, fuller.

"But I'm asking you to think about *how* we grow. About what we keep as we move forward. Because if we trade what makes Marigold *Marigold* for convenience or cash, we don't just lose old bricks and mortar. We lose our story. We lose the places where our children will remember us. Where their children will wish on the same fountain we did."

A hush fell deeper over the room. Even the restless children seemed stilled by something in her tone.

She stepped aside, revealing a simple easel with large printouts of the renderings she'd drawn — by hand at first, then polished for presentation. The same square. But familiar. The original fountain, cleaned and restored. The shopfronts freshened but unchanged in shape, their quirks intact. Flowerbeds brimming. Benches repaired, not replaced. A square that looked like it had been loved into its next chapter, not scrubbed of its past.

"I don't have a million-dollar marketing team behind me," Sophie said, a small, wry smile touching her lips. "I don't have skyscraper investors. What I have is a plan that starts from what we have — and builds from there. With you. With your hands, your stories, your hopes. It'll take longer. It'll be harder. But it will still be *ours*."

She drew a breath, willing herself to be braver than she felt.

"I didn't come back to Marigold to build a monument to myself. I came because I made a promise — to my mother, yes, but also to myself — that the place that shaped me deserved a chance to shape itself. Not be shaped by people who don't know us, don't love us, and won't stay when the shine fades."

And then, from the back, the scrape of a chair. Cal rose.

His voice, when it came, was rougher than usual, but strong. "I've known this town my whole life. I've seen its highs and lows, seen folks come and go. Seen good times, seen hard ones. But I've never seen someone from away work as hard as Sophie Caldwell has — not just to build buildings, but to build *trust*. And that's a damn sight harder. I don't speak for Marigold. No one does. But I'm standing with her tonight."

The hall held stillness like a held breath — one waiting to be let out, one that might, just might, release a tide of hope.

The Debate

For a long beat, no one spoke. Sophie's words seemed to linger in the room like the scent of rain before a storm — soft but full of promise, or warning. Cal's stand beside her had shifted something. You could feel it, like the square itself holding its breath, waiting.

Then the questions came. First, a cautious hand — Mrs. Tolliver, the pantry organizer, her voice steady but anxious.

"How will we pay for this, Sophie? We can't plant hope in empty pockets."

Sophie nodded, grateful for the honesty. "Through grants already in review, historic preservation funds we're eligible for, and small-business incentives we've lined up with partners. And yes, through hard work and patience. I won't promise riches overnight. But I *will* promise that every dollar stays tied to the town's future — not to outside investors' pockets."

A councilman — Mr. Walker, always wary — leaned forward. "And if the grants fall through? What then? Do we stall out while the square rots?"

Sophie held his gaze. "Then we find another way. We scale back, we phase the work, we lean harder on regional partnerships. But we don't abandon it. And we don't sell our future for quick cash."

A ripple of murmurs — approval from some corners, concern from others.

Then came sharper voices. A man in a denim jacket, sleeves frayed, rose from near the back.

"I got a kid who can't find work in this town. I got a mortgage two months behind. Don't stand there and tell me I should wait for some pie-in-the-sky plan when we could have real money coming in *now.*"

Sophie felt the sting of his words — not for herself, but for what they revealed: the desperation under the surface.

Before she could reply, Cal spoke, his voice calm but firm.

"No one's saying your struggle doesn't matter, Jimmy. It does. But what happens when the fast money dries up? When the jobs are gone, and the square's no longer ours? We've seen it happen to other towns. Hell, we've *lived* it. I say we fight for something that lasts."

Jeanine's voice rang out next — sharp as a bell, cutting through the rumble of tension.

"Young folks think old-timers don't see what's coming. But I do. I've seen what happens when you sell a town's soul. This isn't just about jobs. It's about what kind of home we leave behind."

And so it went — voices raised, questions fired, frustrations bared. Sophie answered each with as much honesty as she could summon, admitting where uncertainty lingered, where risk remained. She didn't dodge. She didn't promise more than she could deliver.

Some argued fiercely for the developer's plan — tempted by the shine of new infrastructure, the promise of paychecks.

"It's just business," one man said. "We can't live on sentiment."

But others — especially as Cal and Jeanine spoke, as Sophie's quiet resolve held steady — began to shift in their seats. A woman near the front, tears glinting in her eyes, whispered to her neighbor, "I'd rather rebuild slow, if it means we keep what matters."

The room became a map of human fear and hope: faces etched with longing, weariness, pride, doubt. A town at a crossroads, unsure whether to leap or to stand its ground.

And through it all, Sophie stayed rooted. Not offering perfect answers, but offering truth. And in that truth, something stronger than persuasion: trust, slowly earned.

The Vote Looms

The final question faded into silence, like the last echo of a bell. No one moved at first. The weight of what had just unfolded — the clash of hopes, fears, and hard truths — seemed to press down on every shoulder in the room.

Hester Boyd rose slowly from the council table, her gaze sweeping the packed hall. Her expression was weary, yes — but also resolute, as if she felt the same ache the town did: the ache of choices that would leave someone disappointed no matter how they fell.

She cleared her throat, and even the restless children at the back hushed.

"This council has heard from both sides," Hester said, her voice steady despite the crack of emotion beneath. "We have a responsibility to weigh what's best for Marigold — for today, and for the years ahead."

A murmur rippled through the crowd — tension, expectation, dread.

"We'll meet privately to deliberate," she continued. "A decision will be announced within forty-eight hours — and it will be final."

Forty-eight hours. It might as well have been a lifetime. Sophie felt the number land in her chest like a stone. Around her, the room seemed to exhale all at once — the tight-held breaths, the clenched hands loosening, the murmurs rising as neighbors turned to one another, debating, consoling, speculating.

Some faces were guarded, already retreating into their own private hopes or doubts. Others watched Sophie with something like quiet respect — not agreement, perhaps, but respect for the fight she'd given.

Sophie gathered her notes, though they felt suddenly weightless — as if everything important had already been said, and words alone could carry it no further.

She felt, rather than saw, Cal at her side. No grand gesture, no words yet. Just his presence, solid and certain, like the square's old oak tree: battered by storms, but still standing.

As the hall began to empty, people spilling out into the night, Sophie and Cal remained for a moment. Together, but quiet. Their exhaustion mirrored in each other's eyes. Their bond, unspoken, stronger than ever.

Outside, the air was cool, tinged with woodsmoke from a distant chimney. The square lay in darkness, save for the soft glow of the fountain's single working lamp — a fragile beacon against all that lay ahead.

Cal finally spoke, low enough that only she could hear.

"We did what we could."

Sophie nodded, then allowed herself the smallest smile. "And whatever happens, we did it together."

They stepped into the night together, the weight of the waiting heavy on their shoulders — but shared.

Chapter 17

The Decision

The sky over Marigold felt heavier than it had in weeks, the low-hanging clouds thick with the promise of rain that might or might not come. A breeze rattled the flags on the town hall's porch, the fabric snapping softly in the hush that had settled over the square. Even the birds seemed to have fallen silent, as if nature itself sensed what was at stake.

Sophie paced the worn brick path outside the town hall's front steps, her boots scuffing the moss that crept between the cracks. Every few strides she stopped, rubbed her hands together as if to warm them, then started again. Waiting had never been her strength, especially not when the future — her future, the town's future — balanced on the thin edge of a vote.

Inside, beyond the thick oak doors, voices rose and fell, muffled by plaster walls and generations of paint. She imagined the council members around the battered table, the weight of decisions settling into their bones. What were they saying now? Were they arguing? Were they remembering the faces in the crowd — or only seeing the dollar signs in the developer's proposal?

A sound behind her — the crunch of boots on gravel — made her pause. Cal. He didn't speak as he came to stand beside her, hands shoved into the pockets of his worn work jacket. His gaze followed hers to the doors, then drifted across the square, where the fountain stood dark and still, as if waiting too.

For a long moment, they said nothing. There was no need. His nearness was its own kind of comfort, solid and steady in a world that felt anything but. The square around them, usually so familiar, seemed strange in this hour — the benches empty, the shops shuttered, the lamplight casting long, uncertain shadows.

Finally, Sophie exhaled a breath she hadn't realized she'd been holding.

"Feels like we're standing on the edge of something," she said quietly.

Cal nodded, his jaw tight. "We are."

And together, in the hush before whatever came next, they waited.

Small-Town Rumors & Reactions

The square, usually so full of familiar rhythms — the clatter of dishes from the café, the hum of quiet conversation outside the barbershop — felt fractured now, broken into clusters of hushed voices and worried glances. People lingered in small groups along the edges of Main Street and beneath the overhang of the hardware store, drawn as if by some invisible thread to the place where history might be made, or unmade.

Sophie saw them — neighbors she'd grown up with, strangers who had once been just faces in a crowd but now carried the weight of judgment in their eyes. Some watched her with cautious hope, the kind that dared not speak too loud for fear of jinxing it. Others regarded her with thin-lipped skepticism, arms crossed, eyes sharp, as if bracing for disappointment.

Mrs. Dawkins, planted like a sentry beneath the wide awning of the post office, fanned herself briskly with a folded newspaper — more for effect than for the warm breeze. Her voice carried farther than she perhaps intended.

"I heard they're voting it down. Mark my words — you can't trust outsiders, not with something this important."

Her companion — a wiry man from the feed store — muttered in agreement, but Sophie caught the flicker of doubt in his eyes.

Jeanine's quiet figure moved through the murmuring crowd, a steady current in the swirl of uncertainty. She didn't stop to join the speculation or fan the flames of gossip. Instead, as she passed Sophie, she offered a nod — small, but full of meaning. A nod that said: I see you. I believe in you. Stay the course.

Cal shifted beside Sophie, his jaw tightening at the whispers and at the way even those he'd known all his life seemed caught between loyalty and fear. His hand brushed briefly against hers, not quite taking it, but close enough that Sophie felt the warmth of it, the promise of solidarity in the face of doubt.

Across the square, the church bell tolled the hour. The sound echoed off the brick facades, marking time that felt stretched thin with waiting, with wondering. The whole town held its breath, listening for the creak of the town hall door, for the decision that would chart their course.

And in that charged, fragile quiet, Sophie understood something: it wasn't just about the vote. It was about what people chose to believe — in her, in themselves, in the future they wanted to claim.

Sophie's Doubts Surface

The murmur of the town faded as Sophie turned slightly, her gaze tracing the cracks in the square's paving stones rather than the faces of those watching. The late afternoon light slanted low, catching the fountain's dry rim and turning it to gold. But to Sophie, the square felt hollow — as if the hope she'd tried so hard to build was slipping through her fingers.

Her voice, when it came, was low enough that only Cal could hear.

"I don't know if I can do this." The words tasted bitter, foreign on her tongue. She'd worn the armor of determination for so long that admitting the crack felt like betrayal — of herself, her mother, the town.

Cal's brow furrowed, but he didn't interrupt. He waited — the first person in what felt like forever to give her the space to fall apart without judgment.

Sophie's breath shook as she went on.

"This… this wasn't just about fixing up some buildings. It was about proving I could build something real. Not just on paper. Not just in plans or sketches. But here. Where it matters."

She laughed softly, without humor. "And maybe I was kidding myself all along."

Cal was quiet for a beat, the sounds of the town — the low hum of voices, the rustle of wind through the oaks — filling the space between them.

Then, his voice, rough but gentle.

"I didn't want to like you." The confession startled her enough that she looked up, met his gaze. His eyes weren't guarded now — they were open, vulnerable in a way she'd hoped for but never expected.

"Because if I liked you, I had to believe you could do what no one else could. That this place… that I… we could change. And believing? That scares the hell out of me."

Sophie blinked, the burn of tears she hadn't expected stinging the corners of her eyes. They stood there, two people laid bare by the storm they'd tried so hard to weather alone. And in that fragile, precious moment, something shifted — not the square, not the town. Themselves. The quiet, tentative trust that comes not from victory, but from standing together in the hardest part: the waiting.

The Verdict

The town hall doors stood shut, heavy oak barriers between hope and disappointment. Sophie felt the weight of every second stretch, the hush of the gathered crowd deepening the longer the council deliberated. The sky, streaked with the last blush of evening, darkened to indigo as lamplight flickered to life along the square.

Beside her, Cal shifted his stance, his boots scuffing softly against the worn stone. He said nothing, but the way his shoulder almost brushed hers — steady, solid — grounded her in a way no speech or blueprint ever had.

Then: the creak of hinges. The doors opened, slow as the turning of a tide.

Out stepped Hester Boyd, the council chairwoman, her expression unreadable in the half-light. Behind her, the council members filed out in a line, faces lined with fatigue, with the gravity of their choice. The crowd drew in a collective breath, the kind that tightens chests and stills hearts.

Hester's voice carried across the square, clear but measured.

"Thank you all for your patience." A pause, heavy with meaning. "After careful deliberation, the council has reached a decision regarding the proposals for Marigold's square."

Sophie gripped the edge of her jacket pocket, fingertips brushing worn fabric, knuckles white.

"We have voted to approve the Caldwell preservation plan—" murmurs rippled instantly, some relieved, some questioning "—with the following conditions: regular oversight by a community-appointed committee, quarterly public reviews, and a preservation covenant to protect key historic structures in perpetuity."

A beat. Then Hester added, her gaze flicking to Sophie:

"This isn't the end of the work. It's the beginning."

The square seemed to exhale. Applause broke out — hesitant at first, then warmer, fuller, though not universal. Relief spread like sunlight after storm clouds, mingled with hesitation from those who still feared what change might bring. Sophie heard a few grumbles from those who'd pinned their hopes on big money and fast fixes. But above all, she felt the shift — from uncertainty to cautious belief.

The crowd had begun to disperse, voices low and scattered across the square like the wind carrying autumn leaves. Some townsfolk lingered in small clusters, digesting the council's decision — cautious optimism mixing with the familiar wariness of change. A few shook Sophie's hand, murmuring, "Thank you," or simply nodding as they passed, their faces still uncertain but softer than before.

Sophie stood rooted, heart still thudding against her ribs, the adrenaline of the moment ebbing. She felt hollowed out and full all at once — the paradox of hard-won ground. The square seemed transformed under the glow of the lamplights: the old fountain's shadow long and noble, the boarded windows of the shops no longer symbols of decay, but of possibility.

Cal approached quietly, hands in his pockets, his usual guarded air softened. For the first time since she'd returned to Marigold, his expression held no trace of skepticism — only respect, and something more tender beneath it. His voice was low enough that only she could hear over the hum of departing neighbors.

"Looks like you're stuck with us after all, Caldwell."

The teasing lilt in his tone was there, but beneath it lay something real — an admission that she wasn't an outsider anymore. Not in his eyes.

Sophie's breath caught, the enormity of the journey washing over her. All the plans, the sleepless nights, the doubts — and this simple, unexpected gift of belonging. She blinked rapidly, tears she hadn't intended rising and blurring the square's flickering lights.

"Good," she said, her voice unsteady but sure. "I'm exactly where I want to be."

Cal smiled, small but genuine, and for a moment, it felt like just the two of them in that square — not the plans, the council, the battles, but two people who had fought for something larger than themselves and found each other in the fight.

Without thinking, Sophie reached out — lightly — and brushed a speck of sawdust from his jacket sleeve, a gesture so simple, so intimate it surprised them both. Cal didn't pull away. His hand covered hers briefly, a wordless promise that the hardest part might be over — and that whatever came next, they'd face it together.

A Quiet Resolve

The square emptied slowly, like a tide retreating at dusk. Voices faded. Footsteps echoed on the worn brick paths. Lights in the surrounding buildings blinked out one by one, until only a handful glowed in the deepening blue.

Sophie stood alone, her hands tucked into her coat pockets, the night cool against her skin. The weight of the day settled into her bones — not heavy in defeat, but in the satisfying exhaustion of a battle fought with everything she had.

She let her gaze travel over the square, now quiet but brimming with unseen life. She didn't see the peeling paint or the cracked pavement. Instead, she saw children racing between flowerbeds not yet planted. She saw shop windows lit up with warmth and promise. She saw neighbors pausing to talk over steaming cups of coffee, their laughter mingling with the steady splash of the restored fountain.

And in those imagined scenes, she saw herself — not passing through, not fixing and leaving, but rooted here, part of the town's pulse.

Across the square, the familiar glow of Marigold Books & History caught her eye. Jeanine's light still burned, a single beacon in the quiet. Sophie smiled, warmed by the thought of her ally, steady as ever, working late as she always did when the town's story needed tending.

The breeze stirred, carrying the faintest hint of woodsmoke and autumn leaves. Sophie closed her eyes for a beat, breathing it in. When she opened them again, she felt different. Stronger. Ready.

Tomorrow, the real work would begin. But tonight, she allowed herself this hard-won peace — standing not in a battleground, but at the heart of a home.

Chapter 18

Laying Foundations

Morning broke over Marigold not with fanfare but with a quiet kind of promise. The first light of day crept over the square, gilding the edges of the old brick buildings, glinting off windows that hadn't shone this brightly in years. The air smelled of wet earth and cut grass, a scent Sophie hadn't realized she'd come to love. Today wasn't about speeches or meetings. Today was about hands in the soil, boots on the ground, sweat and effort.

Sophie stood at the heart of the square, blueprints tucked beneath one arm, the other wrapped around a steaming mug of coffee she'd barely tasted. Her hair was pulled back, practical. The jeans she wore were already smudged with dust from an early survey of the site. Around her, small clusters of volunteers and workers trickled in — a mix of curious onlookers, longtime locals who'd doubted but now came to see, and a few steadfast allies who believed. The hum of cautious optimism filled the morning air.

Cal arrived as the sun pushed fully over the rooftops, the soft thud of his boots on pavement announcing him before his voice did. His tool belt slung low, sleeves already rolled to his elbows, he carried the steady, unhurried energy of a man who knew the work ahead would demand everything — and was ready to give it. Their eyes met across the square — not a greeting of words, but of understanding, a silent exchange of *We're here. We're doing this.*

He stopped beside her, surveyed the square with a builder's gaze, then the people with a protector's eye. "You ready?" he asked, quiet but certain.

Sophie nodded, though inside, nerves twisted with hope. "Ready as I'll ever be."

Together, they turned to face the day — no longer cautious collaborators. Today, they were partners, not just in vision, but in action.

The first hammer rang out against a loose plank. A broom swept dust from cracked sidewalks. Someone laughed — the sound bright, unexpected. And so, with the smallest of sounds and the simplest of gestures, Marigold's renewal began.

Community Mobilization

By mid-morning, the square was no longer a place of silence and speculation — it was alive with purpose. The rhythm of work rose and fell like music: the scrape of shovels against packed dirt, the hiss of power washers cutting years of grime from the old brick, the clatter of ladders being positioned against faded facades. The air vibrated with the sounds of renewal, as if the town itself had been holding its breath and was finally exhaling.

Sophie moved among them all — blueprints rolled under one arm, sleeves pushed up, clipboard long forgotten in favor of direct action. She directed crews with a surprising ease, her voice carrying clearly but kindly, adapting on the fly as new challenges surfaced. A pile of debris too large for one group? Sophie organized a chain of volunteers, turning the task into a shared effort that drew laughter as much as sweat. A cracked window overlooked in initial plans? She made a note, promising to find the funds for its repair.

Her eyes met those of skeptical townsfolk as they worked: the hardware store owner who'd grumbled that she was "just another dreamer," now handing out nails and screws at no charge; the widow who'd watched from her porch for weeks, now offering cold lemonade from a fold-out table. The small gestures mattered. Sophie made sure each was acknowledged — a nod, a word of thanks, a smile that felt genuine because it was.

Cal worked in tandem, no longer the reluctant helper but the quiet force of momentum. Where Sophie brought energy and vision, he brought steadiness and practical know-how — showing teens how to reset a crooked fence post, guiding a retired carpenter as they shored up a sagging awning. And when doubt flickered in a volunteer's eyes — when the weight of so much work loomed too large — it was Cal's voice that reminded them: *"One board at a time. That's how we build."*

Sophie noticed it, too — how people looked to him, how they listened. And how, somehow, they were beginning to look to her in the same way.

The square was changing. But more than that — Marigold was beginning to change itself.

A Moment with Emma

The sun had crested high by midday, its heat tempered by a soft breeze that carried the scent of fresh-cut wood and damp earth. Sophie paused at the edge of the square, drawing in a breath she hadn't realized she'd been holding. The morning's progress showed in small but powerful ways: windows glinting clean, flowerbeds turned and ready for planting, brush piles cleared from walkways long hidden.

Needing a break from the swirl of activity, Sophie's gaze caught on a splash of color near the edge of the community garden plot. There, crouched low, was Emma with a paintbrush in hand, a splash of green on her cheek, and a determined furrow between her brows. A wooden sign lay across her knees, the letters *"Marigold Community Garden"* emerging in cheerful green and yellow strokes. Little flowers adorned the corners, bright and hopeful.

Sophie approached slowly, not wanting to interrupt. But Emma, sensing her, glanced up with a shy but proud smile.

"Hey there, artist," Sophie said gently, crouching beside her. "That's beautiful."

Emma beamed. "I wanted it to look happy. Dad says people should feel welcome here."

Sophie's heart swelled. She sat down in the grass beside Emma, watching the careful way she dipped her brush and added tiny petals. The child's focus reminded her of her own mother — of long-ago afternoons spent drawing garden plans in the margins of notebooks.

After a quiet moment, Emma spoke, her voice small but steady. "I miss my mom. But... I like seeing Dad smile again. He smiles more when you're around."

Sophie blinked, caught off guard by the sweetness — and the honesty. She swallowed the lump that rose in her throat. "I miss my mom too," she admitted softly. "And I like seeing your dad smile, Emma. He's a good man."

Emma nodded, as if this were a simple fact of the world. "Promise you'll stay? Even when it's hard?"

Sophie hesitated, the weight of the promise Emma was asking for settling over her. But then she smiled — real and sure. "I promise. No matter how hard it gets."

Emma's grin returned, wide and bright, and she turned back to her painting, humming as she worked. Sophie stayed a little longer, letting the moment soak in — the sun, the breeze, the sound of life returning to the square. And in Emma's small, earnest presence, Sophie felt the roots of belonging sink a little deeper.

Unexpected Setbacks

The sun had begun its slow dip behind the rooftops of Marigold, casting long shadows across the square. The hum of activity had softened— teams packing up tools, volunteers wiping sweat from their brows, laughter mingling with the clatter of folding chairs and ladders. Sophie allowed herself a breath, a fleeting sense of satisfaction as she surveyed the day's progress: planters cleared of weeds, crumbling storefronts now scrubbed clean, and the faint scent of fresh paint still lingering in the air.

But the fragile peace was shattered by the sharp call of one of the local contractors, Mr. Simms—a wiry man in his sixties with hands as gnarled as the oak trees lining Main Street. He jogged toward Sophie and Cal, wiping dust from his face.

"Best come see this," he said, his voice tight.

Sophie's stomach sank. She exchanged a glance with Cal—a wordless exchange they'd grown used to—and followed Simms to the edge of the square where the old mercantile building stood. The structure, a cornerstone of their vision for a revived market row, had always looked worse for wear, but Sophie had hoped its bones were strong enough to save.

Simms pointed to a corner where the foundation met the earth. A large section of brickwork had crumbled away under the day's cleaning efforts, exposing fractured support beams and rot so deep the wood seemed to sag with the weight of decades of neglect.

Sophie crouched, running her fingers along the splintered wood, the grit of decayed mortar crumbling beneath her touch. The weight of it hit her all at once — the cost, the delays, the risk of everything unraveling before it had truly begun.

"This means what I think it means?" Cal asked, though his face already bore the answer.

Simms nodded grimly. "That corner's not just tired — it's on borrowed time. Without serious reinforcement, it won't make it through the next hard rain. And that's before we even start proper work on the interior."

Sophie straightened slowly, brushing dirt from her palms, her mind already racing through numbers: budgets stretched thin, grants earmarked for specific uses, timelines that couldn't bear another major delay.

As if summoned by their vulnerability, the rival developer's representative appeared at the edge of the square — as slick as ever in a tailored jacket unsuited for the dust and sweat of the day. He smiled like a man who smelled opportunity.

"I hear you've run into a little trouble," he said, his tone oily with false concern. "It just so happens we've got resources — crews, capital — ready to step in. This project doesn't have to stall, you know. You could still make this easy on yourself. On everyone."

Cal bristled, stepping forward, but Sophie lifted a hand, stopping him. She fixed the man with a steady gaze, every muscle taut beneath the surface.

"We'll handle it," she said, her voice calm but firm. "Thanks for the offer."

The rep's smile widened a fraction. "Just remember — time is money, and goodwill only stretches so far. Think about it."

He turned and walked away, his polished shoes leaving no trace in the dust he so clearly disdained.

Sophie exhaled, slow and steady, fighting the rising tide of frustration and fear. Cal watched her, his features softening as he recognized the storm behind her composed exterior.

"We'll figure it out," he said gently. "That's what we do. One board, one breath, one day at a time."

Sophie nodded, though the weight of the day felt heavier now. "We have to," she murmured. "There's no turning back."

The square, bathed in the golden glow of dusk, seemed to hold its breath with them, waiting to see what they would do next.

Cal and Sophie Strategize

The old hardware store had become their unofficial headquarters — a place where the dust of history clung to every surface and the creak of the floorboards seemed to echo with generations of plans, deals, and dreams. Tonight, it was lit by a single lamp balanced atop a stack of paint cans, casting pools of warm light over blueprints, receipts, and notepads that covered the battered counter like a patchwork of hope and desperation.

Sophie stood over the mess, one hand braced against the counter's edge, the other rubbing at the tension in the back of her neck. Cal entered quietly, carrying two mugs of coffee — strong and black, the way they'd both come to drink it on nights like this. He set one down beside her without a word.

For a long moment, they didn't speak. The weight of the setback — the mercantile's failing foundation, the rival developer's smirk still fresh in their minds — hung between them. Outside, the square was silent, the kind of silence that made you aware of your own heartbeat.

Sophie finally broke it. "I'm not sure how much more the budget can take, Cal. Even if we strip everything down, even if I forgo my fees, we're still short. And this building — we can't just let it go. It's the anchor to the whole west side."

Cal sipped his coffee, his brow furrowed in thought. "I know. And you're right — it matters. Folks have memories in that place. My dad used to take me there for nails and feed. First time I ever bought something with my own money was in that shop. A pocketknife I wasn't old enough for, but the owner let it slide."

A faint smile touched Sophie's lips at the image, but it faded quickly under the weight of the moment. She turned a page in the blueprint stack, revealing a sketch of the mercantile's façade, her notes scrawled in the margins: *preserve lintel detail, reuse original brick if possible, cost?*

"We could apply for that state emergency preservation grant," Sophie offered, though her tone held little conviction. "It's a long shot, but—"

"Do it," Cal said, more certain than she felt. "Long shots are better than no shots."

Sophie nodded, pulling the grant file from a pile of folders. As she flipped through it, a slip of paper fluttered loose — a printed email she'd tucked away days ago and nearly forgotten. Her eyes caught the sender's name, and her breath hitched.

Dana L. — Regional Revitalization Fund.

She skimmed the message again, heart quickening. The tone had been cautious, yes, but it had ended with: *"If you're able to submit a revised proposal by next week, we'd be open to a second review. There's potential here."*

She passed it to Cal. "Remember the fund that turned us down last month? I got this a few days ago. I wasn't sure it meant anything — but now..."

Cal read the note, then looked up. "It means they're still watching. Still thinking about it."

He leaned forward, tapping a pencil against the blueprint. "I've got suppliers who owe me favors. Maybe I can get materials at cost, maybe even donated. And my crew — we'll work double shifts if we have to."

Their eyes met across the counter, exhaustion mirrored in both, but beneath it — something stronger. Determination. Partnership. Trust, growing in the soil of shared struggle.

Sophie exhaled slowly. "We're really doing this, aren't we?"

Cal's voice was low but sure. "Yeah, Caldwell. We are."

They spent the next hour sketching ideas on scraps of paper, making lists on the backs of old receipts, mapping out a strategy as imperfect as it was earnest. The smell of sawdust, coffee, and ink filled the air — the scent of a town's rebirth, in progress.

At one point, Cal's hand brushed Sophie's as they reached for the same pen. Neither pulled away immediately. The spark was there, real and undeniable, but tonight, it didn't need words. Tonight was about the work, about building something bigger than either of them alone.

Outside, the square lay quiet under a quilt of stars, but inside the store, plans were being laid — foundations stronger than brick beginning to set.

A Night Beneath the Stars

The night air outside the hardware store was cooler than Sophie expected

— the kind of crisp, clean air that carried the scent of sawdust, damp earth, and the faintest trace of honeysuckle from somewhere down the block. She stepped out onto the sidewalk, arms folded loosely across her chest, the weight of blueprints and budget sheets briefly forgotten.

The square lay before her, touched by moonlight, transformed by effort. Earlier that day, it had bustled with voices and tools, laughter and strain; now it was a canvas of quiet promise. The edges of buildings softened in the silver glow, their scars hidden for a time, their potential shining through. Even the fountain, still dry and cracked, seemed to gleam as if remembering what it once was.

Sophie drew a slow breath, feeling both the exhaustion in her bones and the hope in her chest — fragile, but growing stronger.

A creak of the hardware store door behind her. Cal joined her on the stoop, tool belt slung over one shoulder, sleeves still rolled, the lamp's warm glow behind him casting him in silhouette. For a long moment, neither spoke. They simply stood together, taking it in.

His shoulder brushed hers, light at first, then steady, as if the touch was no longer accidental. Sophie didn't move away.

"It's strange," Cal said softly, his voice blending with the night. "Standing here, looking at this square… I always thought I'd spend my life trying to protect what was left of it. Never imagined I'd be part of building something new."

Sophie turned to him, seeing the honesty in his face, the quiet wonder that hadn't been there months ago. "You are building something new," she said. "We both are. And it's real, Cal. No matter how hard they try to stop us — this is real."

He hesitated, then nodded, as if letting himself believe it. "We're building something real here. I didn't think it could happen. But now… I do."

Her answer was simple, but it carried everything she felt. "Me too."

The night stretched wide around them, stars sharp against the velvet dark, the square below balanced on the quiet fulcrum between memory and hope. There were still battles ahead — they both knew it — but for this moment, they stood together, grounded, certain.

A promise beneath the stars.

Chapter 19

The Storm Before the Bloom

Marigold woke beneath a low, heavy sky, the kind that seemed to press down on the roofs and tree limbs, thick with the promise of a storm. Sophie stepped onto the square just as the first breeze stirred the early summer heat, her boots crunching against the gravel path where weeds had been cleared only days before. The place she had begun to think of as a canvas for hope now felt strangely hollow — like a stage after the actors have left, the final applause long since faded.

She paused, the weight of sleepless nights and uncertain days heavy on her shoulders. The square was quiet in the way that small towns are just before something breaks loose — not peaceful, but braced. She sipped her coffee, the bitterness doing little to sharpen her thoughts. And then she saw it.

Graffiti.

Black spray paint, fresh enough to glisten in the morning light.

KEEP MARIGOLD OURS

The letters were large, uneven, slashed across the newly painted wall of the old hardware store — the very wall Sophie had stood beside only a week earlier, arms aching with the effort of scrubbing and sanding decades of grime and neglect from its brickwork.

The words hit harder than she would have expected. She stared at them, the coffee forgotten in her hand, heart beating in her ears. There was no signature, no way to know who had done it — but the message was clear. Clearer than any council vote or whisper campaign: **You don't belong.**

Sophie stepped closer, as if proximity would somehow soften the impact. She touched the edge of a letter, fingertips grazing the rough spray of paint. The blackness seeped into the cracks between bricks like a stain that would never wash clean.

Across the square, a shopkeeper swept his stoop, casting glances at her when he thought she wouldn't notice. A woman walking a small dog crossed to the other side of the street. Two teenage boys on bikes slowed just enough to take in the sight before pedaling off, whispering behind cupped hands.

The whispers started to rise, carried on that rising breeze that smelled of rain.

"I heard they're selling the square to outsiders."

"Big city deals — never ends well."

"She's not one of us, no matter what she says."

Sophie drew a breath, willing the sting in her eyes to stay put. She had known this wouldn't be easy. She had expected resistance. But knowing and feeling weren't the same, and standing here now, facing the scar across their shared dream, the distance between her and this town felt wider than it ever had.

Behind her, the morning noises of Marigold stirred: a screen door creaked open, the clatter of dishes in a café kitchen, the faint buzz of an old radio playing a hymn she hadn't heard since childhood. Life, going on, even as the fault lines beneath it deepened.

Her gaze swept the square — the fountain still dry and cracked, the benches half-sanded, the planters waiting for soil and seeds. All the pieces of hope she had tried to set in motion. Were they only ever hers? Had she mistaken politeness for acceptance? Did these people see her as anything but an outsider with big ideas and a knack for stirring trouble?

A sudden gust lifted the ends of her hair, flapped a loose sheet of blueprints pinned to the hardware store window. Yesterday the square felt full of possibility; now it seemed fragile — too easily broken.

And yet, beneath the humiliation and the doubt, something else stirred. Anger. Not hot, reckless fury — but the steady kind. The kind that comes when you know someone has misunderstood your heart, and you refuse to let that stand.

Sophie wiped her palms on her jeans, squared her shoulders, and turned from the wall. She didn't yet know how to answer the message, but she knew one thing: it wouldn't be the final word.

Cal's Frustration

Cal heard the argument before he saw it — sharp voices cutting through the quiet morning like a sawblade through soft wood. He set down the crate, wiped his hands on a rag from his pocket, and stepped around the café. His boots scuffed against the brick as he rounded the corner, the tension in his chest tightening with every step.

A small knot of townsfolk had gathered by the café's side door: three men he'd known his whole life, shoulders hunched like they were bracing against a storm, and Hester Boyd's cousin Irene, arms folded, mouth drawn tight. Their voices lowered a notch when they saw him, but the resentment lingered in the air like the smell of burnt coffee.

"Morning," Cal said, keeping his voice steady. His gut told him to turn around, to leave them to their grumbling. But this was his town. His square. He wasn't about to walk away.

One of the men, Martin Crane — whose family had run the feed store for generations — was the first to speak. "We were just talking, Cal. About how some folks seem to think they know what's best for the rest of us."

Cal crossed his arms. "That so?"

Irene's eyes flashed. "You can't tell me you're blind to what's happening. She comes in with big plans, makes a few speeches, and now we're all supposed to hand over what's left of this town's soul?"

Cal clenched his jaw. He wasn't a man who liked words used carelessly, and "soul" was a heavy one to throw around. He took a breath. "Sophie's not here to take anything from Marigold."

"Oh?" Martin said. "What do you call those big city plans she keeps pushing? What do you call that graffiti this morning — folks are angry, Cal. They're scared. Maybe it's time you stopped siding with someone who doesn't belong."

That last part landed like a punch. Cal felt heat rise in his neck. He thought of Sophie standing in the square at dawn, her face pale but her eyes steady, staring down that hateful scrawl. He thought of how she'd rolled up her sleeves alongside them all, how she'd listened more than she'd talked, how she'd fought for the square not for herself, but for all of them.

And he thought of the fear in Martin's voice — the kind that had nothing to do with Sophie at all, but with losing the last threads of what made this place home.

"She does belong," Cal said quietly, surprising even himself with the certainty in his voice. "More than some folks who've lived here their whole lives and forgotten what it means to fight for this town."

That earned him a hard stare from Irene. "You'd choose her over your own?"

"I didn't say that." Cal ran a hand through his hair, the frustration simmering beneath his skin. "But I won't stand here and listen to you tear her down just because she's trying to help."

The group fell silent, the tension thick as the clouds overhead. A breeze stirred, carrying the scent of honeysuckle and fresh-cut grass, softening nothing.

Cal felt the weight of his words settle heavy inside him. Because the truth was, he did understand. He understood the fear of change, the pull of promises that sounded too good to be true but were easier to believe than the hard, slow work of fixing what was broken. He understood wanting to protect what little they had left, even if it meant shutting out someone who might actually care.

But he also knew what it felt like to stand still for too long, to let fear dictate your choices until the place you loved faded into something you didn't recognize. And he wasn't about to let that happen. Not now.

"I'm not looking for a fight," Cal said, his voice low. "But if you want to have this out, don't do it behind folks' backs. Say what you mean, out in the open. Like we used to."

He turned before they could answer, the rag in his pocket forgotten, fists clenched at his sides. The square lay ahead of him, quiet now but thrumming with all the things unsaid. And somewhere in that square was Sophie — trying, despite everything. And somehow, that mattered more than his own comfort, more than their doubts, more than the fear that tugged at him from both sides.

Cal kept walking, boots striking a steady rhythm on the uneven sidewalk, knowing the storm had only begun.

Sophie Doubts Herself

The hardware store smelled faintly of sawdust, oil, and old paper — comforting scents once, but now they clung to Sophie like reminders of how far she felt from certainty. The midday sun streamed through the cracked windowpanes, casting stripes of gold across the scuffed wooden floor and the scattered blueprints spread before her. She sat cross-legged on the ground, fingers absently tracing the lines of a design that suddenly seemed naive in its optimism.

Stacks of reports and invoices surrounded her like a fortress she couldn't escape. The numbers didn't lie. The hidden structural damage to the west building would cost nearly twice what she'd budgeted — money they didn't have, promises she wasn't sure she could keep. And outside these walls, Marigold was turning on itself. The graffiti that morning, the whispers Cal had described when he came by earlier, the looks from townsfolk that once held hope but now brimmed with suspicion. It felt like everything she'd tried to build was crumbling faster than she could patch it together.

Sophie drew in a shaky breath and leaned her head back against the cool wall. Once the heart of the revival, the hardware store now felt like the belly of a sinking ship.

Her gaze landed on a battered notebook near the edge of the worktable. The leather cover was cracked, the spine frayed from years of handling. Her mother's notebook. Sophie reached for it, hands trembling just slightly. She opened to a random page, and there, in her mother's looping script, was a passage she'd read a hundred times before, but that hit her now like a balm and a blade all at once.

"A town is not its buildings. It is its people, and what they choose to protect when times get hard. When fear creeps in, that's when you see a town's true heart."

Sophie closed her eyes, feeling the sting of tears she'd been holding back since dawn. *What if Marigold's heart didn't want what she was offering? What if all her sketches and plans, her long nights and early mornings, had been for nothing? What if she was forcing a future on this place that it didn't want — couldn't bear?*

The hardware store door creaked open, the sound startling her. She wiped at her eyes, steeling herself, expecting Cal or perhaps one of the volunteers. But it was Jeanine, carrying two steaming mugs of tea and wearing that look that said she'd seen right through Sophie's walls from the first day they met.

Jeanine set the mugs down and settled on the floor beside her without a word at first, simply taking in the chaos of papers, the tired slump of Sophie's shoulders. Finally, she spoke, voice gentle but edged in truth.

"Looks like you're drowning in good intentions," Jeanine said, nodding at the mess.

Sophie let out a bitter laugh. "That's about right."

Jeanine handed her a mug. The tea smelled of mint and something earthy, grounding. "You think you're failing," she said, not as a question.

Sophie stared down at the tea, watching the steam curl like smoke signals from a fire she couldn't put out. "I don't know what I think anymore. Maybe I was arrogant to believe I could do this. Maybe the town doesn't want saving. Maybe I'm just trying to finish something because I promised my mother I would — not because it's what Marigold really needs."

Jeanine's gaze softened. "Let me tell you something about promises. They aren't about getting it perfect. They're about showing up. Again and again. Especially when it's hard." She leaned closer. "And real change? It always meets resistance. If it didn't, it wouldn't be change. It would be convenience."

The words sank in slowly, like rain into dry ground. Sophie swallowed hard, the knot in her throat easing just a little.

"I don't know if I'm strong enough," she admitted.

Jeanine smiled — not a wide grin, but the quiet kind that holds steady against storms. "You already are. Because you're still here."

Sophie looked around the hardware store again, seeing the same cracked walls and battered furniture, but through a slightly clearer lens. The work wasn't over. The doubts wouldn't vanish overnight. But maybe — just maybe — that was what made it worth it.

She straightened her shoulders, fingers tightening around the warm mug. The storm outside was still gathering. But inside, Sophie felt something anchor deep — a promise not to herself, not even to her mother, but to the town that hadn't yet decided whether to believe in her.

A Vulnerable Moment

Night settled heavy over Marigold, the kind where even the air held its breath. Outside, the square lay quiet and still, the lamplight casting long, golden pools onto the cracked sidewalks and shuttered storefronts. But inside the old hardware store, a single bulb glowed above the worktable, illuminating the scatter of papers, sketches, and notes like relics from a battle still being fought.

Sophie didn't notice the door creak. She was too deep in the numbers, wrestling with the tangle of costs and timelines that had taken over her life. A pencil was tucked behind one ear, her hair a mess of loose strands she hadn't bothered to tame since morning. She stared at her mother's notebook, open to a page she'd read a dozen times that day, the words blurring under the weight of exhaustion.

Then came the familiar sound of boots on wood — steady, measured. She looked up, startled, to find Cal standing there, framed in the doorway, the square's shadows clinging to him. His eyes softened as they met hers, and for a moment, neither spoke. The silence wasn't awkward — it was full of things they hadn't said yet.

"I saw the light on," Cal said quietly, stepping inside and closing the door behind him. His voice was low, as if he didn't want to break the fragile stillness of the night.

Sophie tried to smile but couldn't quite manage it. "Burning the midnight oil, I guess. There's always more to figure out."

She shook her head, this time not in despair, but in something quieter — uncertainty laced with guilt. "I'm starting to wonder if I promised the wrong things. Or to the wrong people."

Cal's brow furrowed. "What do you mean?"

"This whole time, I've been trying to finish what my mom started. To do it her way. The blueprints, the speeches, the town halls…" She looked up, her voice low. "But what if Marigold doesn't need another revival plan? What if it needs something I haven't even let myself imagine?"

Cal leaned forward, something shifting in his gaze. "Then maybe it's time to stop chasing someone else's dream and figure out what yours looks like. You've earned that."

She studied him — the weight in his shoulders, the steadiness in his voice. "And if I get it wrong?"

"Then we fix it," he said simply. "Together."

Cal's hand shifted slightly, as if he meant to close the space between them, but he stopped himself. The weight of the moment, the town's fate, their own unspoken fears — it all held them back. Instead, he offered her what he could.

"We'll face it together," he said, voice steady now. "Whatever comes next."

Sophie nodded, swallowing past the lump in her throat. "Together."

And in that quiet, flickering light, with the storm still gathering beyond the walls, they sat side by side — not quite touching, not quite speaking — but no longer alone.

Rival Developer's Play

Dawn broke gray and cold — the kind of morning that crept in quietly, like it didn't want to be noticed. The square was still, but not peaceful. It felt… paused. Like a breath held before a punch.

Sophie crossed the bricks with coffee in hand, scanning the shopfronts. She almost missed it at first — the deliveries weren't dramatic. No banners, no fanfare. Just *placement* — quiet, surgical, everywhere.

Packets at every doorstep. Brochures tucked neatly under doormats, wedged between door handles, pinned discreetly to corkboards. Not the noisy blitz from weeks ago — no rally, no loud promises. This was targeted. Intentional. Calculated to look like a formality, not a campaign.

She picked one up. Heavy stock. Embossed. Clean. Familiar branding, but now with a subtle twist: the renderings were smaller in scale, less sweeping, more "integrated." Page three held the headline: **"Focused Renewal: A Shared Vision for East Marigold."** A single block. A "pilot phase." A *proof of concept.*

Her stomach turned.

It was brilliant — in a way that made her skin crawl. The plan didn't scream takeover anymore. It whispered *compromise.* A smaller footprint. Just a test. Just a taste. Something town leaders could approve without admitting surrender.

She imagined the pitch: "Let's just try it. No harm in seeing what progress looks like."

Across the square, she caught movement — Hester Boyd, packet in hand, lips pressed tight. Further down, a young shop clerk flipped through the glossy pages with genuine curiosity. A council member stood with the developer's rep on the corner, nodding along to whatever was being said.

Jeanine appeared beside her like a shadow. "They're not selling a vision," she said. "They're selling division."

Sophie didn't speak. She didn't have to. She could feel it happening — the shift. No longer a fight over ideals, but a campaign of erosion. Of quiet concession.

By midday, the council notice confirmed it: a bid had been submitted for redevelopment of a portion of the square. Not all of it. Just enough.

Sophie stared at the words, the coffee in her hand forgotten. It wasn't retreat. It was infiltration. And it was working.

"This isn't a new offer," Jeanine murmured. "It's a wedge. And if they get it through…"

"They won't stop there," Sophie finished.

She folded the packet, tighter than she needed to, and turned back toward the hardware store.

This was no longer just about saving buildings.

It was about holding the line.

Under the Same Stars

Night fell slowly over Marigold, the kind of soft descent that seemed to hush even the most restless hearts. The square, so tense with division by day, now lay bathed in moonlight and the glow of porch lamps and streetlights. The air was cooler, carrying with it the faint scent of honeysuckle and the memory of rain that never quite came.

Sophie stood at the edge of the square, near the fountain that had become a kind of anchor for her. Its basin was dry now, the water pump offline for repairs, but she imagined it as it would be—clean and flowing, catching moonlight in ripples of silver. She let the quiet seep into her bones, willing it to drown out the swirling doubts, the whispered fears she'd heard all day.

Behind her, the hardware store's door creaked open, and footsteps approached. She didn't have to turn to know it was Cal. His presence was steady, like the earth beneath her feet—solid, reassuring, complicated.

He stopped beside her, Close enough to feel his warmth, close enough that if she leaned, their shoulders would brush. But she didn't move, and neither did he. For a long moment, they just stood there in silence, two figures beneath the same sky, watching over a town teetering on the edge of something vast and unknown.

Finally, Cal broke the silence, his voice low and rough with the weight of the day. "Looks different at night, doesn't it?"

Sophie nodded, not trusting her voice just yet. She breathed in the night, the mingling scents of sawdust, wildflowers, and the faintest trace of Cal's soap.

He glanced sideways at her. "You holding up?"

She let out a breath that was half-laugh, half-sigh. "Barely."

"That makes two of us."

For the first time in what felt like forever, Sophie allowed herself to be vulnerable in his presence—not the determined project leader, not the architect trying to save face, but just Sophie. A woman tired to her bones, fighting for something she believed in, afraid of losing it all.

"I keep thinking," she said quietly, "maybe I'm trying to force this town into something it doesn't want. Maybe I should step aside and let them take the easy road."

Cal shook his head. "No." The word was firm, unyielding. "You've done more for this town than anyone's dared in years. You reminded us what it means to care."

Sophie looked at him then, really looked. In the moonlight, the lines of worry on his face softened. There was no armor in his gaze tonight, no guarded distance. Just a man as scared as she was, and as stubborn about fighting for what mattered.

"Whatever happens," he said, his voice gentler now, "we don't quit. Not on the town. Not on each other."

The last words hung between them, electric and fragile all at once. Sophie's heart thudded in her chest, the promise in his voice threading through the cracks of her doubt like a lifeline.

"Not on each other," she echoed, her voice steadier than she felt.

And for the first time in days, the weight on her shoulders felt a little lighter. Not because the battle was over—it was only just beginning—but because she wasn't standing at the edge of it alone.

They stood a while longer, watching as a breeze stirred the banner strung between two lampposts: Marigold Rising. The words felt both a memory and a promise.

Sophie let the stars steady her, even as her mind circled the day's cruel truth — the rival hadn't backed off. They'd just changed their play, making it harder to say no without seeming small.

Above them, the stars blinked to life, one by one, scattered across the velvet sky. Sophie tipped her head back, drinking them in. The same stars her mother had wished on from this square. The same stars Cal had watched on nights when everything felt lost. The same stars that had watched over Marigold through every storm.

Tonight, they watched over two fighters, two hearts learning trust, two souls daring hope.

Under the same stars.

Chapter 20

The Vote

The council's special meeting dawned gray and heavy, as if the sky felt the weight of what was coming. Clouds loomed low over Marigold, casting a muted pall over the town. The air was still, that breathless quiet before a storm.

Sophie stood at her window, mug of coffee cooling in her hands, staring down at the square. From this vantage, she could see it all: the empty benches waiting for neighbors to gather, the flag at half-mast from some old commemoration, the fountain's silent basin, the storefronts that bore the scars of years of neglect and months of hope.

But what she saw most were the signs of division—banners in shop windows, subtle but telling. Some bore hand-lettered slogans — Save Our Square, Marigold Strong — nodding to her vision. Others, glossier and more polished, sported the rival developer's sleek logo, promising *A New Marigold for All.*

The square was no longer just the town's heart; it was the battleground for its soul.

Below, townsfolk began to gather. They came in twos and threes at first, wrapped in jackets against the chill, their voices low and wary. Sophie could see Mrs. Dawkins gesturing animatedly, no doubt spreading her usual brand of pessimism. She caught snatches of conversation when she opened the window a crack:

"—heard they'll sell us out, just you wait."

"—Sophie means well, but is that enough?"

"—better jobs, better roads. What's so bad about that?"

Each word felt like a pebble in her shoe: small, irritating, painful in accumulation.

She set the mug down and pressed her forehead to the cool glass. For months, she'd poured herself into this town, into this dream. And now, it felt like the ground was shifting beneath her feet, as uncertain as the sky above.

Across the square, the town hall's steps filled with bodies. People she'd come to know—the café's barista, the barber with the crooked smile, the kids who sketched murals on scrap paper, Cal's crew with their work-worn hands—all gathered now, divided in their hopes.

The mayor arrived, flanked by council members, Hester Boyd among them. Hester's expression was unreadable as she climbed the steps, but Sophie thought she caught the faintest flicker of sadness in the older woman's eyes.

The rival developer's team arrived next: crisp suits, confident strides, clipboards in hand. They shook hands with familiar faces, smiled at nervous townsfolk, exuded the polished charm of people who'd done this before—and won.

Sophie's heart pounded. She knew that charm, that easy confidence. She'd seen what it left behind: towns stripped of character, their hearts hollowed out in the name of progress.

"Time to go, Caldwell," she thought to herself.

Outside, the cold hit first. Then the weight of all those eyes. Conversations faltered as she crossed the square. Some people nodded, offering hesitant smiles. Others looked away, as if unsure what to make of her, this outsider who'd dared to care.

Cal stood near the hall's entrance, arms crossed, jaw tight. Their eyes met, and for a beat the noise of the crowd faded. His nod was small, but it steadied her more than any speech she could have given herself.

Together, they climbed the steps. Together, they would face the storm.

And above them, as if watching, the clouds gathered darker still.

Jeanine's Quiet Strength

The morning light filtered through the narrow streets of Marigold like a soft promise, but Sophie barely noticed. Each step toward town hall felt heavier than the last, her pulse drumming a frantic rhythm in her ears. The square, usually a place that grounded her, felt strange this morning— tense, watching, waiting. The cobblestones, the storefronts, even the fountain's broken rim seemed to hold their breath along with her.

Sophie had rehearsed a dozen variations of what she might say today, but each felt thin against the weight of what was at stake. Once again, the rival developer's money, the promises of instant jobs, the lure of "progress"—all of it hung over the town like a storm cloud ready to break.

She adjusted the strap of her bag on her shoulder and kept her gaze straight ahead. That's when she spotted Jeanine.

The bookseller stood at the edge of the square, where the sidewalk narrowed between the café and the florist's closed-up shop. Jeanine wasn't hurrying like the rest. She stood with a stillness that seemed at odds with the restless energy around her. In one hand she held a battered leather tote, as if she'd just come from an early errand. A striped scarf was looped around her neck, the ends fluttering slightly in the breeze.

Jeanine saw Sophie coming and stepped forward. There was no hesitation, no fuss. Just Jeanine — steady, unflappable. The kind of woman whose calm could settle a room, or, Sophie hoped, a heart.

They met near the lamppost where someone had tied a ribbon weeks ago during Square Revival Day. The ribbon had faded now, frayed at the edges.

Sophie opened her mouth, but Jeanine raised a hand gently, forestalling any attempt at conversation. Instead, she reached out and took Sophie's cold, tense hand in her own. Jeanine's fingers were warm, firm, grounding.

"Trust what you've built here," Jeanine said softly, her voice carrying easily despite the murmuring crowd that swelled behind them. "People see it, even if they don't always say it."

For a long moment, Sophie couldn't speak. The words weren't grand. They weren't a rallying cry or a guarantee. But somehow, they were exactly what she needed.

Jeanine's gaze held hers, clear and unwavering. There was something fierce in it—a reminder that quiet strength could be the strongest of all. And in that brief connection, Sophie felt something inside her steady. The fear didn't vanish. The doubts didn't evaporate. But Jeanine's faith anchored her, even as the storm of uncertainty swirled.

Sophie gave a small nod, squeezing Jeanine's hand back. "Thank you," she managed, her voice thick.

Jeanine smiled—just a small quirk of her mouth, but filled with meaning. She didn't offer more words. She didn't need to. With that, she stepped back into the crowd, vanishing into the throng like a stone dropped into water, ripples lingering in her wake.

Sophie stood for a moment longer, the echo of Jeanine's words settling in her chest. Then, squaring her shoulders, she turned toward town hall. The building loomed ahead, its steps crowded, its windows gleaming in the morning sun. A symbol, like everything else today, of what might be lost—or won.

As she climbed the steps, she felt Cal's presence before she saw him. He waited at the top, watching her with a look that was both a question and a promise. She didn't answer either with words—just a glance, steady and sure.

And together, without speaking, they stepped into the building.

Inside Town Hall

The air inside town hall was thick — not just with the scent of old wood and floor polish, but with tension so sharp Sophie could almost taste it.

The grand double doors groaned shut behind her, muffling the restless hum of the crowd still gathering outside. But inside, the room was anything but silent.

Voices overlapped in low murmurs; the scrape of folding chairs echoed off the high ceiling. The town hall's walls, lined with faded photographs of Marigold's past — parades, ribbon cuttings, Fourth of July picnics — bore witness to the moment. Sophie felt the weight of that history pressing down as she stepped further in, Cal just behind her.

Every seat was taken. People stood packed along the back and sides of the room, spilling into the aisles. Sophie recognized nearly every face: shopkeepers who'd once doubted her, farmers who'd offered lumber for the clean-up, parents she'd chatted with at the café, teens who'd planted flowers in the square. And among them, the skeptics — the ones who'd nodded politely but kept their distance, the ones who'd whispered that maybe Marigold didn't need saving after all.

Near the front, reporters from a regional paper scribbled notes, their cameras ready, waiting for whatever would unfold.

Sophie drew in a slow breath, the notes she'd clutched so tightly in her hand now crumpled at the edges. The room felt too small for so many people, so much hope and fear crammed together.

The mayor called the meeting to order, voice louder than necessary, as if volume could mask his nerves. Then, with an almost theatrical flourish, he introduced the rival developer's team.

Sophie's stomach tightened as they took the floor — three men and one woman, tailored and poised, but this time, something was different. Their leader, tablet in hand, didn't stride in with the bluster of conquest. He arrived like a trusted consultant, a partner, someone already halfway in the door.

There was no dramatic unveiling, no flashy music or theatrical lighting. Just a quiet hum of authority as the projector flickered on. The slides were simpler now — no sweeping skylines, no high-rise fantasies. Instead: a few tidy blocks, softened color palettes, benches with discreet branding, a rendering of a modest café nestled beside a repaved walkway. The aesthetic wasn't grand. It was familiar. Approachable. Designed to disarm.

He spoke with the calm confidence of someone who'd been watching, listening. "We understand Marigold isn't looking for reinvention," he said, voice even. "You're looking for relief. Stability. A partner who respects your roots — and helps you grow from them."

Jobs were mentioned again, but this time with local names. Small business grants. Selective restoration. Words like *shared ownership*, *public-private partnership*, *community incentives*. It wasn't a takeover. It was a seduction.

Sophie felt the shift in the room. This wasn't a repeat of the last pitch — it was its evolution. More targeted. More believable. And more dangerous. Because this time, they weren't offering to change the town. They were offering to *be part of it*.

And yet, beneath the veneer of respect, Sophie saw the truth: the core hadn't changed. There was still no mention of Marigold's past. No space for memory, just a curated version of what outsiders might find quaint. It was still a plan to overwrite — only now, with subtler ink.

Sophie scanned the room. Some faces were alight with interest, drawn to the lure of quick prosperity. Others shifted uneasily, glancing toward neighbors, trying to read the room. Cal stood near the wall, arms crossed, jaw tight — watching both the presenters and the townsfolk, as if weighing every reaction.

And Sophie?

She felt the tight knot of worry in her chest ease — just a fraction. The developer's team finished to polite applause, their smiles tight, their eyes already turned to the council members seated at the dais.

The mayor glanced at Sophie. "Ms. Caldwell?" he said.

Sophie rose. Her notes were in her hand, but her mind was already beyond them.

As she walked to the front of the room, she felt something shift —
not certainty, not yet. But resolve.

She stepped up to the lectern. The hum of the room softened. Her
fingers touched the edge of the wood. She took one breath, then another.

Now it was her turn.

Sophie's Final Plea

Sophie stood for a heartbeat in the space between the council's table and
the crowded room, feeling the weight of all those eyes on her. The
crumpled notes in her hand suddenly felt irrelevant — too small, too
rehearsed, for what this moment required.

She set them down on the lectern without looking at them. She
didn't need them. Not anymore.

She took a slow breath, feeling the hum of the old building's
creaking timbers beneath her boots, the warmth of bodies packed into
every seat, the electric tension hanging between hope and fear. And when
she spoke, her voice wasn't loud — but it carried.

"As you heard me say before, I could stand here and tell you
numbers. Timelines. Budgets. I could try to outshine their slides with
prettier pictures."

She let that sink in, scanning the room. Some eyes stayed wary, arms
crossed tight. But others... others softened, leaning in just a little.

"But no, all I want is for you to remember what matters here —
what made Marigold *ours*. And I've seen that. In your stories. In your
work. In every hand that helped clean up the square, every neighbor who
shared coffee and doubts and hope. This town isn't broken. It's waiting
— for us to choose what kind of future we want."

"Their plan — it's shiny. It's fast. It might even bring in money, for
a while. But it asks us to trade who we are for what we think we can get.
It erases Marigold so it can sell us something new. They're going for part
of the square today — and the rest won't be far behind."

A murmur rippled through the crowd. Sophie felt her heart hammering, but she pressed on.

"Our plan isn't as fast. It asks for more of you — more patience, more heart, more trust. But it gives something back, too. A square where your children will know the stories behind the bricks. Where visitors will come not because we look like everywhere else, but because we look like *Marigold*. Where we don't lose ourselves in chasing dollars — we build on what's already ours. Look at the progress we have made since the last vote by this council."

She paused, swallowing the lump that rose unexpectedly. "I can't promise perfection. But I can promise this: I'll be here. I'll keep showing up, as long as you'll have me."

A hush fell. Even the usual coughs and chair scrapes seemed to stop.

The room stayed silent for a beat — then someone clapped, hesitant at first. Then more joined in. It wasn't thunderous, not yet. But it was real.

Sophie felt her knees want to give, but she stood tall. Not because she was sure of victory — but because, in that moment, she was sure of herself.

She had spoken the truth. And now, the town would decide.

The Vote

The applause from Sophie's plea faded slowly, like the last notes of a song no one wanted to end. The room settled into a tense, charged silence — a breath held by an entire community.

Hester Boyd, the council chair, cleared her throat, the sound loud in the hush. She looked out at the crowd, at Sophie, at Cal, at the rival developer's polished team seated near the front. Her gaze lingered on Sophie a second longer than the rest.

"Well," Hester said quietly, "we've heard both sides. We thank you all for your passion. Now the council will deliberate."

The council members pushed back their chairs, the scrape of wood on wood sharp as a rifle crack. They filed out of the room into the small anteroom behind the dais. The door shut with a soft but final click.

And then, the waiting began.

The room seemed to exhale at once — whispers rising like steam. Sophie let herself sag for just a second, resting her hands on the lectern's edge. Cal stepped closer, his presence a quiet shield.

"You did good," he murmured.

"I don't know if it's enough," she admitted, voice barely above a whisper.

"You said what needed saying. That's all any of us can do."

Minutes stretched. The sky darkened, streetlights flickering on one by one. Inside, the air grew thick — with heat, with worry, with the weight of what might come.

The rival developer's rep conferred in low tones with his team, glancing toward the dais door with a smile.

Sophie caught that look and felt her stomach twist.

At last, the door opened. The council filed back in — faces guarded, expressions hard to read. Hester took her seat at the center of the table, her hands folded tightly on the worn wood.

"This hasn't been an easy decision," she began, her voice carrying to the farthest corner. "Both proposals offer potential. Both come with risks. We weighed them carefully."

Sophie stood very still. Cal's hand hovered at her back, as if ready to steady her if she swayed.

"The vote will be by roll call," Hester said. "Councilor Walker?"

"Aye — for the Caldwell plan."

Sophie's heart lurched.

"Councilor Martinez?"

"Nay — I believe the developer's proposal is more secure."

A knot tightened in Sophie's chest.

"Councilor Green?"

"Aye — for Caldwell."

"Councilor Abernathy?"

"Nay."

Two and two. The room was utterly silent now, the kind of silence that makes you feel your own pulse in your ears.

Hester drew a breath, met Sophie's gaze. The chair's vote would decide.

"Aye — for the Caldwell plan. It's time we trusted our own."

The room seemed to explode — not in wild cheers, but in heartfelt applause born of relief, of shared release. Some clapped, some just sagged against their chairs, some wiped at their eyes.

Sophie let out the breath she hadn't realized she'd been holding. Cal turned to her, eyes bright, and without thinking, he pulled her into a fierce, brief hug.

"You did it," he said into her hair.

We did, she thought.

As the applause began to subside, Sophie felt movement beside her. The rival developer's lead representative stepped forward — the one whose smile had never quite reached his eyes.

He extended a hand.

"Well played, Ms. Caldwell," he said. "I don't agree with the vote — but I respect how you earned it."

Sophie hesitated only a second before taking his hand. His shake was firm, brief, and gone before she could read too much into it.

He gave a small nod — something between concession and calculation — then turned and walked out with his team, their crisp suits now just part of the evening's shadows.

Hester rapped the gavel once for order. "The motion passes, with conditions: community oversight, regular reports, and a preservation covenant on historic structures." She met Sophie's gaze. "You have our support. Use it well."

Sophie nodded, tears threatening but held at bay.

And as the crowd began to stir, to file out into the night, she knew: the hardest work was still ahead.

But for the first time, she believed they could do it — together.

Aftermath

The crowd spilled out of town hall like a tide released, voices rising, mixing relief, exhaustion, and lingering debate into the night air. The square — so long still, waiting — now hummed with new energy.

Sophie stood on the top step, blinking as if the world had shifted beneath her feet. She felt unmoored, caught between the weight that had just lifted and the enormity of what lay ahead.

Cal was beside her, close enough that she felt the heat of him in the cooling evening. For a heartbeat, neither of them moved, as if afraid that doing so might break the fragile magic of the moment.

Then he turned to her, his voice low so only she could hear. "Looks like you're really stuck with us, Caldwell. This time for good."

The words undid her. Sophie felt the sting of tears, unexpected and unstoppable. She managed a shaky laugh. "Good. I'm exactly where I still want to be."

They stepped down together, into the square that felt at once familiar and new. Neighbors clapped them on the back, offered handshakes, promises of help. Even the grumpiest shopkeeper lifted his cap in a small salute. Children chased each other along cracked sidewalks, their laughter ringing like a promise.

Sophie's gaze found the fountain, its cracked bowl and stubborn weeds no longer a symbol of loss, but of what could be rebuilt. Cal followed her look, and together they crossed to it.

The lanterns swayed gently, casting pools of amber light. The square had never felt so alive.

Cal's shoulder brushed hers, grounding her. "Guess it's official. You're one of us now."

"Finally," Sophie whispered.

Cal drew a slow breath, his gaze searching hers. Sophie answered in the only way that felt right. She closed the last inches between them and kissed him — fierce, sure, full of all the weight of the fight, the relief, the hope.

When they parted, breathless, he rested his forehead against hers. "Together," he said.

Sophie nodded, heart full. "Together."

Around them, the square quieted at last, lanterns glowing low. The fountain stood as the first stone in the foundation they'd build — not just for Marigold, but for themselves.

And as they turned at last toward home, hand in hand, the square behind them bathed in starlight, Sophie felt not fear, but promise — bright, steady, and real.

A Place Called Home

The fountain bubbled, its soft splash mingling with the hum of conversation and the sweet notes of a fiddle drifting from the makeshift stage. Sunlight glinted off the water, and for the first time in decades, coins sparkled at the bottom — not forgotten wishes, but promises kept.

Sophie stood at the edge of the square, watching as Marigold came alive around her. Children darted between vendor booths, faces sticky with ice cream. Old-timers lounged on benches freshly painted in the town's colors, trading stories that drifted on the breeze. The scent of barbecue and fresh bread mingled in the warm spring air.

She drew a slow breath, the kind that filled her to the brim. This was what her mother had dreamed of — what she had fought for. Not just buildings restored or streets repaved, but a community finding its heart again.

"Penny for your thoughts?"

She smiled, turning toward Cal. He looked good — relaxed in jeans and a button-down, sleeves rolled up, sawdust still clinging to his boots. His hand found hers, their fingers threading easily together.

"I was thinking she'd be proud," Sophie said quietly.

Cal followed her gaze to the fountain, where his daughter, Emma, tossed a coin with solemn care.

"She would," he said. "And she'd be proud of you."

Sophie leaned into him, letting his steady presence hush the last of her doubts.

The past year had been a whirlwind — storefronts reopened, feuds laid to rest, friendships forged. Harder than she'd imagined. Better, too.

Emma ran up, cheeks flushed, eyes bright. "I wished for a puppy," she announced, grinning.

Cal groaned, but Sophie laughed. "We'll see, kiddo."

Jeanine appeared, a plate of cobbler in hand. "Don't let him off the hook, Emma. This town could use a proper shop dog again."

The three of them laughed together, and Sophie marveled at how natural it felt — this belonging.

Home wasn't just where you were from. It was where you chose to stay — and where you dared to build. Cal squeezed her hand. "Ready for the ribbon cutting, partner?"

"Ready," Sophie said. And she meant it.

Emma tugged Sophie's sleeve. "Can I help cut it?"

Sophie glanced at Cal, who gave an approving nod. She crouched to Emma's level, smiling. "It's yours too, kiddo. You helped build it, whether you know it or not."

Sophie placed her hand over Emma's small one, guiding it to the handle of the oversized scissors. Cal rested his hand on top of both.

As the mayor stepped to the mic and the crowd quieted, Sophie took one last look at the square. The banners. The music. The faces full of hope. The scars hadn't disappeared — they never would. But they'd healed. And in their place, something stronger had taken root.

Marigold wasn't just a town on a map anymore.

It was hers. Theirs. A promise kept.

And as the ribbon fluttered to the ground, Sophie couldn't help but wonder what came next — for Marigold, for herself, for all the places still waiting to be called home.

About the Author

Cameron Lane writes stories about second chances, transformation, and the unseen forces that shape our lives. Best known for heartwarming small-town romances, Cameron's work also explores deeper journeys of spirit, resilience, and mystery — always with emotional depth and a belief in the human capacity to rebuild.

Whether in the familiar streets of a struggling town or at the edge of the unknown, Cameron's characters seek connection, truth, and home.

When not writing, Cameron enjoys wandering the unfamiliar, collecting traces of heritage, and reflecting on the spaces where light meets shadow.

Book Club Discussion Guide

1. What does the title *The Squaring of a Heart* mean to you after finishing the novel? How does it reflect Sophie's journey—and Marigold's?

2. Sophie returns to Marigold to fulfill her mother's dream. How do her memories of her mother shape her decisions and sense of purpose?

3. Cal is often quiet and reserved, but his presence is central. How does his emotional arc unfold through the story, and what does his relationship with Emma reveal about him?

4. The town square becomes almost a character in its own right. What does it represent to different members of the community? To you as a reader?

5. Discuss the generational dynamics in the novel—between Sophie, her mother's memory, Jeanine, Emma, and others. How do these relationships impact the story's themes of legacy and change?

6. How does the novel handle the tension between progress and preservation? Were your sympathies ever divided?

7. There are many subtle "rebuilt" relationships—romantic, familial, communal. Which did you find the most satisfying or surprising?

8. If you were in Sophie's shoes at the start of the book, would you have stayed in Marigold? Why or why not?

9. How did the presence of the developer and external pressures deepen your understanding of what Marigold represented to the characters?

10. Which scene or moment resonated most emotionally with you? Why do you think it had such an impact?

11. How did the author's descriptions of Marigold and its people influence your connection to the town and story?

12. What lasting impression or message did you take away from the novel? Has it changed or reinforced your views about community, heritage, or personal growth?